LAUREN NEWBROOK

Wildfire

There's no one more dangerous than a mother under threat

Copyright © 2024 by Lauren Newbrook

All rights reserved. No part of this publication may be reproduced, stored or transmitted in any form or by any means, electronic, mechanical, photocopying, recording, scanning, or otherwise without written permission from the publisher. It is illegal to copy this book, post it to a website, or distribute it by any other means without permission.

This novel is entirely a work of fiction. The names, characters and incidents portrayed in it are the work of the author's imagination. Any resemblance to actual persons, living or dead, events or localities is entirely coincidental.

First edition

This book was professionally typeset on Reedsy. Find out more at reedsy.com

*For all those around me who give me strength and love
and for those no longer with me, who gave me more than I knew*

"A mother's love for her child is like nothing else in the world. It knows no law, no pity, it dares all things and crushes down remorselessly all that stands in its path."

- Agatha Christie

Wildfire
[waɪld.faɪər]
noun

1. A raging, rapidly spreading fire.
    i. Uncontrolled
    ii. Often in rural areas
    iii. Highly flammable, difficult to extinguish
2. Something that acts very quickly and intensely.
3. Lightning occurring without audible thunder.

1

"Please just get your shoes on!" Exasperation punctuated her every word. "Please Alfie, we're going to be late. Just leave the stone on the stairs, it'll still be there when you get home," she pleaded.

Alfie hadn't always been his name, but she'd come to prefer it to his original one. Less conspicuous—there must be four other Alfie's in his year group alone. Her name hadn't always been Nicole either.

They left on time—just. And began the 20-or-so minute walk to the nearby infant school, Darby Infant and Nursery, in the middling town of Twynesham, somewhere relatively nondescript in the middle of the middling northern coastal region of Norfolk. The walk was always quiet, for pedestrians tended to avoid the narrow path along this road into town, preferring to take the slightly longer route past the high school. This route was only really used by cars, the occupants focused on the road ahead and not bothering to trouble themselves with a mother and child hastily marching to school—she liked it that way.

They crossed over into the school grounds, perfectly timed with the last Monday school bell of the year. As Nicole stopped short of the group of parents standing beneath the tree, she kissed Alfie goodbye and waited while he made his way over to the other five-year-olds lining up for the teacher. She allowed herself to peruse the parents and grandparents, seeing but hardly noticing who was with whom, who stood alone like her, who was eagerly waiting for the arrival of Mrs Rowland so that they could make a hasty retreat to get to work on time, who was clearly more willing to mingle and loiter and catch up with other like-minded parents before starting their day, who looked friendly—who didn't. She glanced back towards Alfie, standing second in line, and he blew her a kiss just as Mrs Rowland beckoned them all inside. She blew him one back and turned to leave, a fraction earlier than all the others, and led the way back out of the school gate. *God that boy melts my heart.*

Nicole was still relatively new to the town. Kept much to herself. She and Alfie were able to relocate here with relative ease, it being his first school and not having any other family to speak of. Nicole had her pick and she chose Twynesham.

The town was just far enough away from the coast to be passed over by most holidaymakers and second-home owners and yet close enough to the larger city of Blyworth to allow for easy access to larger shops and establishments. The average age of Twynesham residents must have been near to 70, another tick in the pro's column. Nicole was drawn to the sleepiness of the town; she could stay anonymous, left alone.

They had been here a couple of years already and although her savings had allowed her to purchase a small cottage on the edge of the town, those funds would soon dry up. Her mission today—as Alfie's was to learn his split-digraphs—was to find a source of income. She walked towards the town square hoping to find an advert in the window of one of the many small independent shops. She took a meandering route around

1

town and the streets stemming off the market square—nothing. There were none. Three charity shops wanted volunteers, but that wasn't going to put food on the table.

She even inquired in both pubs—a tad on the desperate side as it would hardly be keeping low-key if you're serving goodness knows who—but even they didn't have anything going. She was considering the logistical possibilities of making it to the neighbouring town as she caught sight of her reflection in the large plate-glass window of Twynesham Library. Nicole wasn't remarkable to look at—everything middling. A middling woman, in a middling town. Her height was average, her build the same, her hair could be described as dark blonde some days and light brown on others. She wore glasses, although the lenses were only glass. Her clothes were one size bigger than she really was, and today supported a Joules-esque boat-neck striped navy top with "mum" jeans, white plimsolls and an over-sized tote bag. Middling.

Her eyes refocused on the A4 sheet of headed paper blue-tacked to the inside of the window. It was perfectly framed by her dark top. There was a library assistant role available—part-time, flexible working a possibility and a decent wage. She didn't really want to have to apply for anything in such a formal way, cash-in-hand would obviously be far better, but needs must. And she'd always kind of fancied working in a library—recalling childhood dreams of being Belle. Swinging from library ladders and spending every waking minute reading were replaced with the more recent thoughts and desires of wanting a "normal" job. She decided she would apply and made a note of the website address on the back of an old receipt she found in her bag.

As she walked home she thought about the content of her CV—the one she was going to have to concoct once she got back. "*What would they be looking for? Who should I be?*"

2

Gail Pemberton was listening attentively as Sophie spoke. At least Sophie believed that she was. But then, Sophie supposed, all therapists had to listen attentively—or pretend that they were. No, Sophie definitely believed Gail was listening to her and had been for many months now. It was such a shame that this one person, the only person who Sophie had ever bared her soul to, was very soon going to be completely inaccessible to her.

This was her last session. And after today, Sophie could no longer schedule appointments with Gail and build on the valuable work they had accomplished together so far. Sophie was moving away and Gail was contracted out for this—six months of bi-weekly sessions was all the HR policy allowed, and today was the last.

Gail Pemberton was a motherly sort—softly spoken with a soothing tone. Sophie always thought of her as a human sloth—never moving or speaking too fast and with soft, droopy, kind eyes.

"I can see you've progressed such a long way since we first met Sophie."

Sophie gave a lopsided smile by way of a reply.

"It's been wonderful to see how well you've adapted to your

new situation and I really do wish you well. I'm sorry we can't carry on all this hard work. Is there anything specific you'd like to cover in today's session before we finish? We have about 20 minutes left."

Sophie looked around the familiar room and tried to think. She was conscious that her time was running out and she wanted to make the most of it but there were so many things she still wanted to share with Gail and work through; how could she possibly pick one to unpack and discuss in 20 minutes?

"Not really, no. I feel considerably more able and confident in myself and my abilities... and hope I can retain and recall everything you've taught me when I next need it. I think I can."

"I know you can Sophie. I know you can. I really do wish you well, you've been through more than any one person should ever have to deal with in a lifetime, and you're still so young. I hope the move goes well and you settle in nicely."

Sophie gave her another lopsided grin—she found it hard to hear nice things like this.

Gail continued, "Just please don't shut people out. It's so important that you talk to people and make connections with people and I know you find it hard to trust right now..."

"I'll do what I can," Sophie interrupted, desperate for these platitudes to stop.

The pair said their professional goodbyes and, as Sophie stood to gather her jacket and bag, Gail Pemberton crossed over to her treasured Danish teak desk beside the window. She had to write up this last session report and get this case closed— she'd already gone over and above the allowance afforded in the policy. However, this case was too important to dismiss in so few sessions. Gail had pleaded tirelessly to her supervisor about the case and about Sophie—desperate to get them both

2

more time; Gail was granted more time, but it had to be on her own dime.

Sophie moved across to the door and said a final "Bye" to Gail before walking out into the colourless corridor beyond. Sophie had confided in Gail, completely and absolutely. Everything. She'd laid her heart bare and Gail had scooped her up off the floor with her words and nursed her back to a point where she could envisage a life—a normal life.

Sophie stepped out into the fresh post-rain air and took a deep breath.

Gail submitted her final report.

3

Well, this was all turning out nicely. The hours were fitting in around school pick-ups and/or dinner-times with ease, the fellow library assistants and the duty manager weren't too bothered to get to know her in any more depth than the obligatory, "Where are you from?" and "You got any kids?"

She'd been working there for two months already and had shared approximately seven pieces of information about herself: name, age, Alfie's name and age, his school, no other family, and living locally.

The work itself was marvellous—exactly what Nicole was after. She could immerse herself in the quiet, soporific surroundings of the local library and keep herself to herself. Conversations never extended into probing or unwanted territory, which is so often the case once colleagues have worked through all the usual topics of conversation. The visitors only ever wanted to ask her about a reserved book, or to request one not available in this branch, or that the self-serve machine was playing up. Ahh the self-serve machine—what a glorious invention for the introvert... and those in the business of avoiding human contact.

That said, things had been ramping up a tad over the past few weeks. As with all local government departments these days, the library service had to make savings, cut staff or increase capital. There are only so many staff you can cut before you'd have to close the library altogether, so finding ways to maximise commercial income became the hot topic. The library took up the whole ground floor space of a three-storey building, with flats above. Pretty standard fare for a noughties-built block of flats—red brick, concrete parking area around the back and cheap UPVC windows looking out over the market square. The library's main room was open plan with movable bookshelves organised into three neat rows extending towards the back of the space. Along the back, you could find the kids' section, with low-level seating and a table, situated beside the back office door and over-sized photocopier. The clunky free-to-use computers were housed at the front, beside the windows—which as a lifelong screen user didn't seem like a sensible location to Nicole. The glare from the south-east facing windows meant that the vertical blinds were nearly always closed, giving the sense that the place was forever shut. But then this suited Nicole.

What didn't suit Nicole was how the open space between the bank of computers and where the shelves began was the only logical place to "rent out" for gatherings such as book club meetings, craft and hobby classes or even "events" for lonely people to join together and sit in the same place for an hour and just natter. Nicole certainly wasn't so mean-spirited that she didn't want people to socialise and find companionship, she just didn't want them to do it right in front of her desk.

Today's class of choice was a felting workshop where the assortment of ladies (and they were always all ladies) were attempting to copy the tutor's perfectly proportioned penguin which no doubt she had spent *many* hours curating into the most darling cute baby penguin no more than five inches high, sitting on a stack of books in the centre of the round table, proud and straight.

As the second hour approached its end, the offerings ranged from slightly wonky versions of the same, but with unhappy-looking faces or droopy eyes, through those that wouldn't even stand up, to completely unrecognisable black and white pompoms with barely a face at all. Most of the attendees took their leave, pocketing their creative wares and pulling on their coats as they finished up their conversations with their newfound acquaintances. One went for a mooch along the bookshelves, seemingly wishing to avoid leaving at the same time as everyone else. Another made for the desk.

"Hello my woman, hev my book come in yet?" Nicole was asked, in the most delightfully and broadest Norfolk drawl she'd heard yet. This elderly lady must have been pushing ninety but was sprightly enough, with bright, sharp eyes and sporting a most audacious, over-sized cerise scarf.

By way of a greeting, Nicole smiled back and asked, "What was the name please?" in a most dutiful way.

"My name? I'm Iris—Iris Rawlison." Although with the accent Nicole wasn't sure whether it was Rallison, Rawlison, Rollison? Either way, it started with an R—as good a place as any to start. Moving towards the reserves shelf, she asked, "Which title was it?" in an effort to narrow down her search (there appeared to be a few in the R section on the shelf).

"That wus..oh what wus that called agin.. that were a laarge prent carpy of *Staarter f' Ten*—thas f' moy book club."

Nicole found the title immediately—the largest book on the shelf—and placed it on the counter. Dear old Iris had placed her ample handbag on the other side of the counter and was elbow-deep in loose tissues, presumably in search of her library card. She chatted as she rummaged. "Hev you bin workin' hare long?"

"A few months."

"Owh well then, you mus' be roight use't to ol' codgers like me takin' ages to find anyth..." her voice trailed off as she pulled from the bag her bright blue library card. "Hare!" She sounded triumphant.

A genuine smile escaped from Nicole—she found herself developing a real soft spot for Iris. She felt an innate warmth and partiality to her, which struck her as unusual at first as she'd never had a soft spot for anyone at all before (other than Alfie of course)—no attachments, no distractions, no leverage. That was the mantra.

Nicole and Iris continued their transaction, although it hadn't escaped Nicole's keen attention that the fellow felter who hadn't left with the others was edging slowly closer to where they stood. Although this other woman was feigning interest in the books in front of her, Nicole doubted that Teen Fiction was really the section she was interested in.

Iris's dulcet tones snapped her attention back. "I said, I do hate when that rain, don't you?" Mrs Rawlison had been slotting her large book into her shopper and Nicole realised she'd zoned out for a moment.

"Oh certainly, Mrs Rawlison."

"Call me Iris," she said, smiling brightly as she tied her transparent rain hood under her chin, carefully tucking in the front curls of her perm. "Look a'ter yurself now, cheerio!" She collected up the handles of her many bags and turned to leave.

"Bye Mrs—I mean, Iris. See you soon."

Nicole looked straight back to the Teen Fiction section—no

one there. She kept her eyes on the shelves as she walked from behind the desk and glanced down each row as she traversed the library floor, searching for the lone customer. It was time to close up and she needed to make sure the place was empty before doing so. Once, her predecessor had apparently locked up and left while an elderly gentleman was still in the toilet. She'd been in a hurry to get somewhere and hadn't realised anyone had gone back there. Nicole certainly couldn't afford such attention should she make the same error.

She took the time to search more diligently, berating herself and her paranoia. There was no one left behind, no hidden nooks or crannies, no place left to search. She flipped the lock on the front doors and got on with the now-familiar close-down routine.

It was time to get home to Alfie.

4

It was nearing Hallowe'en; the days were short and although Nicole missed the lighter evenings where she could still take Alfie over to the park before dinner, she preferred the dark. Nighttime was better in many ways; hats, scarves and bulky coats hid your features, and the rain-prone weather meant umbrellas would hide what little there was left to show and helped avoid eye contact. Comings and goings weren't as often witnessed, as people stayed in, snuggling on the sofa watching second-rate seasonal flicks on whichever streaming service was the flavour of the month.

Work had ramped up considerably. There were cuts—as predicted—and Nicole's superior career history gave her the edge over the other part-time library assistant. Perhaps she should have felt guilty about that, but then things were going well and Nicole really didn't want anything to change. For the first time in her life, she'd slowed down and had started to enjoy a normal life. And by God didn't she deserve it?

The reduction of staff, though, had meant a slight jiggle around of her hours, and now she was also solely responsible for the social media presence in the local community forums. This wasn't actually as bad as it sounded—Nicole could now have an online presence but under the anonymity of the library page. This was good. It gave her access and insight to people around town without having to branch out with a fake individual account and potentially encourage friend requests and the like.

She was getting towards the end of her shift; the lights were all on as the sun had set an hour ago, the overhead strip lights reflecting on her computer screen making the text tricky to read. She was just adjusting the tilt on the monitor when she became aware she was being watched. She felt the eyes before she could figure out where they were. She frowned as her eyes darted around the room trying to place them. She spotted them—lower down than she'd presumed—and a wide grin split across her face. Alfie!

"BOO Mummy!" he yelled as he jumped out of his hiding place and ran to embrace her. His cuddles were the best. Nicole looked up into the face of Hayley, a fifteen year old girl who lived three doors down and who was the most discreet babysitter she could find. The innocence of a mild-mannered, teenage girl was far easier to trust than a potentially meddlesome older sitter; she was far less likely to gossip to other mums and residents of the town. Hayley explained that Alfie wanted to see Mummy at work so she thought it wouldn't hurt to come along and choose some new reading books for Alfie to improve his phonics.

"It's so good to see you my little pickle," Nicole said as she breathed him in. Pulling back from him to look at his face, she added, "Shall we let Hayley go home and you stay here with me?" The boy nodded eagerly and fell into her for another cuddle. Nicole picked him up as he did so and let Hayley knock off early. She'd still pay her for the unused hour—provided she didn't make a habit of this.

4

Hayley left and Nicole set up Alfie on a big beanbag with a large picture book about a dinosaur that eats everything and then poos everywhere.

She headed back to the desk to finish off the social media post about a new club that would soon be using the library space to hold bi-monthly meet-ups for the Norfolk faction of the UK Roundabout Appreciation Society.

How on earth do I make this sound enticing? '*Come* **around** *to our way of thinking and join us for a bi-monthly deep dive into the beauty of these otherwise humble circular intersections. Meet fellow enthusiasts and one day you might get to meet the President—The Lord of The Rings.*' Oh help. Nicole sighed.

She hit *Post* and began to lock up. Part of this daily ritual included shutting down the public computers. One of them was seriously old—even older than the other really old computers. They might have all had an upgrade to Windows 10 but this one was still ticking along with Windows XP, as its sole purpose was to liaise with the ancient Canon printer. Any more upgrades would mean having to ditch both and the costs were too high for this inconsequential library branch. The XP operating system still rocked the screensavers where you could write a message and have it dart about the screen banging into the edges like a demented pigeon refusing to land. This PC's screensaver usually portrayed the asinine, "A library doesn't need windows. A library is a window." The irony of this statement being on a computer, using Windows, situated right next to an actual window, was always amusing to Nicole. But today it delivered a different message.

"978-0-06-088730-8"

A bit odd. It looked like an ISBN—an International Standard Book Number. This was a unique thirteen-digit code that every published book displays, telling you what country it was from, the language it's printed in and the version of the book. Nicole's first thought was that it was somehow copied and pasted in from someone's book search, but book searches weren't done on that PC which was just for printing. Besides, regular users weren't permitted access to the control panel settings.

Nicole was about to hit the spacebar to log in as administrator when she was startled by Alfie appearing right beside her. "Mummy can we go now?"

"Yes little pickle, Mummy's just got to do a couple more things. You finish your book and I'll be right there."

"I'm finished already," he replied, with more whine in his tone than Nicole would normally tolerate.

"Here, play this for a minute." She unlocked and handed Alfie her smartphone—always a fail-safe when you just need those couple of extra minutes unhindered.

She turned back to the computer screen and punched in the password. Nicole was no stranger to computers. Although her most recently typed CV would have you believe that she obtained a BA in Historical English Literature and was certified by CILIP (Certified Institute of Library and Information Professionals), the truth was far closer to a Masters of Science in Advanced Computer Forensics, with another in Criminology and some additional studies in Sociology, Religion and Linguistics.

There would be no trace of such alterations to a normal admin, but Nicole was straight into the hard coding of the operating system and could bring up and scroll through millions of rows of code in seconds, highly capable of sifting through

4

and finding the exact moment this screensaver was updated. The code generally looked untouched but there was an anomaly which caught her eye.

Thankfully it hadn't happened that many days ago so she didn't need to search for long to find it—last Tuesday at 16:29. She scribbled down a couple of pieces of pertinent information, including the ISBN, and returned the computer to its previous state of inactivity but with a new book-related quote bouncing about the black screen:

...there is no enjoyment like reading...

5

Alfie tucked up in bed, Nicole set about starting her own bedtime routine—a routine that had become so second nature, she had it down to a fine art. She'd get Alfie to bed—he was a good sleeper—then she'd travel from room to room checking each for anything out of place and that the windows were all secure. She'd take her time doing this, moving silently from room to room knowing exactly where to tread to avoid even the slightest creak from a loose floorboard. This gave her the ability to detect all the sounds around her, identifying each one in turn and checking them off her mental list.

She went first to the spare room at the back of the house. The first sound to reach her ears was the gentle rustling from the trees in the back garden. The leaves dropped weeks ago but the bare branches and twigs rubbed together in the wind, the frame still standing proud. The sound of someone retrieving their wheelie bin and taking it back through their garden gate. She moved to the bathroom as that sound ended abruptly. The neighbour—bin back in place—slammed their back door and she heard the five-point locking mechanism shift into place as they wrenched the handle skywards. Nicole liked that sound.

She made sure the bathroom window was locked and stopped to listen again. The boiler was directly below her here and she could hear the low-frequency sounds it made as it kept the heating ticking over on this cold night. Avoiding the middle of the bathroom threshold, she moved silently in socked feet towards her own room at the front of the house. Again, she stopped to take in the surroundings and make sure everything was in place.

A noise.

A click.

Hardly a sound at all. But out of place.

Another sound—rustling. She swivelled her head to locate it.

The front door. Her heart went into overdrive and she noiselessly, but surprisingly deftly, made her way downstairs to confront the source of this sound. As she arrived at the bottom step she stopped to take stock again.

A metallic spring sound.

The outside light was on—that must have been the click—and no sooner had she thought this than a rolled up newsletter was crammed through the letterbox followed by a few fingers. The newsletter hit the mat, the fingers snapped back and the letterbox clanged into silence. It was the local rag, *Only Twynesham*, which ironically covered Twynesham *and* the surrounding areas in about an eight-mile radius. She closed her eyes, willing her heart to slow, and the foreboding panic to dissipate.

Nicole stooped to collect it from the mat as she listened to the retreating footsteps, followed by another letterbox clang as the neighbours at Number 57 received their copy. She glanced at the cover; staring up at her was a beady-eyed close-up of a pigeon with the local church spire in the background and the headline: CHURCH UNDER ATTACK FROM PIGEONS. Nicole idly turned to page four for the rest of the story as she walked towards the kitchen.

> The vicar of Twynesham's St Agnes' Church has spoken for the first time today about the problematic birds that are roosting in the spire of the 14th century building.
>
> The church repairs programme of works is under threat as pigeon droppings have created a health and safety nightmare. The slippery and disease-ridden mess created by the dozens of pigeons roosting there is building up and preventing workmen from accessing the guttering and drains that are in urgent need of repair. This is causing excess rainwater to seep into the church walls.
>
> Plans for a "pigeon guard" were submitted to the town council and it is hoped that this will discourage the roosting spots so favourable to the flying attackers. Details on what a "pigeon guard" consists of are currently open to speculation.
>
> Cllr Neville Barnes said, "I don't know what the church is going to do to fix this but we must stop the menacing pigeons from invading the church roof as soon as possible. My suggestion was to shoot them all but the town council didn't like that idea much."

This was followed by an advert for the local Butchers—Hoxton's—urging customers to: *Get your Christmas meat orders in as soon as possible* and highlighting a special offer of four-bird roasts... the second of the four being pigeon.

Nicole continued checking the ground floor of the house,

stopping, listening, checking and moving on, all without further interruption or incident. She started to make a decaf tea and continued to idly flick through *Only Twynesham* while she waited for the kettle to boil. Other news from around the area included the What's On list of events; the Harvest Festival at the church, the Christmas light switch-on celebrations next month, a new craft taster session—this time Macramé—and news on the *Stars of Tomorrow* featuring the main cast of the High School's Christmas panto. The kettle was done boiling and she poured her tea. Her thoughts returned to the ISBN on that library screensaver. She was working Tuesday afternoon— in fact the time that screensaver was updated coincided with the end of that felting workshop. She couldn't recall seeing anyone at the computer desks but then she was focussed on a delivery of reserves that had come in, and then Iris.

She opened her laptop—a self-built behemoth. This laptop was built and structured to allow her complete and uncompromising control over everything. There would be no trace of her even owning a laptop and she was a mere seven keystrokes away from being able to obtain anything she liked on the darkweb. She was untraceable. She was untrappable. She was safe here. Nothing a computer or website or code could throw at her would be in the least mysterious. She knew everything—hell, she'd developed practically every firewall and cyber-security protocol out there, all based on tech she'd developed whilst still in University.

She opened a search engine—again, of her own design and making. No one was going to capture *her* search history. And she punched in the ISBN, sipping her tea as she did so. The book associated with that ISBN was *Pretty Little Liars* by Sara Shepard. Its bright yellow cover and script cover font monopolised the left side of her screen. She read the synopsis:

> EVERYONE HAS SOMETHING TO HIDE—ESPECIALLY HIGH SCHOOL JUNIORS SPENCER, ARIA, EMILY, AND HANNA
> In ultra-trendy Rosewood, Pennsylvania, four beautiful girls are hiding very ugly secrets. High school juniors Spencer, Hanna, Aria and Emily have grown apart since their best friend Alison DiLaurentis went missing three years ago.
> But now someone is sending them anonymous notes, threatening to reveal their darkest secrets.
> There's only one person who knows that much about them, but Ali's gone...isn't she?

"Threatening to reveal..." Nicole's tiny voice trailed off into the empty room. Sitting completely motionless, brow furrowed and still holding her cup, Nicole wrestled with the idea that this was a direct threat to her. That was her initial reaction, sure. But why? More importantly, who?

An old, familiar, unwelcome feeling reared up inside her. Her well-trained brain forced her heart rate to slow and her breathing to calm, allowing her the space to properly consider the facts and situation. *Don't get carried away, Nicole.* She was here, in this quiet and slow town. She was here with her son. Her son was too young to know anything other than the new reality she had created around him. So who could know? She was so damn careful. But someone had figured it out. Or had they? Had they really?? *It's just thirteen numbers on an old screensaver for fuck's sake. Get a grip, Nicole.*

She took a slurp of tea—it was getting cold already.

Pretty Little Liars. A teen, coming-of-age kinda story. Teen fiction. Iris. The mysterious older woman loitering close by in *the teen fiction section...* Nicole allowed these thoughts and images to percolate a moment. She could visualise the pieces of information and thoughts as separate jigsaw pieces. Her brain was trying each piece against another to see how well it fitted. But there was a fog, too, getting in the way and not letting the pieces come together. She loathed this fog. Too many months had been spent consumed by it in the not-so-distant past.

Her tea was stone cold now but her mind was made up. She'd sit on it and gather more intel, keeping a more vigilant eye and seeing where things landed. She was not going to jump to conclusions.

Maybe she was imagining connections where there were none.

Maybe it was all in her head.

6

It wasn't all in her head.

Two weeks had passed before she found the first one. A makeshift bookmark—merely a scrap of paper—sticking out the top of a book. It was noticeable as this book had been pulled from the neat rows and placed horizontally across the tops of the others.

At first, she assumed that this was due to some lazy borrower pulling it from the shelf and not bothering to slot it back in its place. So much so, she'd almost just tidied it away and had started to screw up the paper when the writing on the page had jogged a memory. She held the book in her left hand as she used it as a block to smooth the paper back out with her right. Written along the top was the same ISBN she'd searched before—the numbers seared into her memory now, much like someone's jackpot-winning lottery numbers might be. But the book she now held bore no relation to *Pretty Little Liars*. She looked at the rest of the note. Under the familiar ISBN was written:

Alea iacta est.
9871448134212

She moved away the note to look more closely at the book it had been left in. *Emma* by Jane Austen—an edition found only in the extensive Classics collection the central library held, all printed in the mid-60s. They rarely saw these old editions in this small library; only ever upon request.

Holding tight to both items she crossed with purpose and composure to the desk. She opened Spydus and punched in this new ISBN. The name Spydus amused her immensely; it sounded so clandestine.

The result was an eBook—a John Grisham. She liked John Grisham but she hadn't heard of this one. She read the synopsis—something about a residential home in Clanton, a new employee coming in, targeting the lonely and wealthy, working his way into their wills whilst uncovering bad practice and then benefiting from the out-of-court settlement. *What the heck has that got to do with Emma?*

The various jigsaw pieces weren't building up a decent enough picture yet. She turned back to the copy of *Emma*. The pages were yellowed and smelled like an old bookshop. She turned the book over in her hands looking for a clue, for something more. She now wished she hadn't whipped the scrap of paper clean out of the book—the page it was tucked in might have formed a valuable steer.

The spine was broken in well—the book being much read. The front sported an image of a regency portrait: a young woman with big brown doe eyes and a simple white empire line gown. A watermark from a wet mug formed a ring that cut across her cheek. The corners were dog-eared and—hang on—there was a page turned down. She opened the book—the well-worn book spine allowing the pages to flop open easily as she looked at the title page for Chapter 42. Written very lightly in pencil in the margin (which surely everyone knows not to do in a library book) was the notation: *Meet on p41.*

She dutifully followed the breadcrumbs and turned to page 41. The first two words she noticed on that page were *Mr Knightley.* She read on, in fact she read back a page to give her some context. Mr Knightley was a character first introduced on page 41. Was this what the notation meant? She was flicking back to Chapter 42 when she was interrupted by a pair of teenage girls who were trying to borrow a DVD but didn't have any means of payment for the self-serve machine. She left the note and book on the desk and went to assist them.

The library was getting busy now that schools were out. She'd have to figure out these clues and meanings later at home when she could really think. Her priority right now was checking if there were any more messages for her before her colleague tidied up tomorrow. She grabbed a stack of returned books that sat next to the self-serve machines and under the pretence of wandering the shelves to put them away, she rigorously searched each and every row. She'd come across another discarded book—but no note. Placing a Bake Off cookbook back on its rightful shelf, she spotted another—tucked right up against the end of a row in the non-fiction section. It was a copy of *The GCHQ Puzzle Book* and although it had a note tucked into page 87, there was nothing written on it. Completely blank. She turned to the back pages of the book—a book she knew so well—and read through the contributors' names. Fourth one down. A name she hadn't seen written or spoken aloud in years. She slammed the book closed.

She checked both books out under her own library card and placed them in her bag, desperately trying to ignore the alarm rising up inside her.

I'll get to you two later, she thought, and walked off to deal with the jammed photocopier.

7

"No. I think you'll find on the day in question, I was briefed at 0900. Before that I was unaware of the situation."

"That is quite simply not good enough. How could you allow such a valuable asset to be used in a deep cover operation? The fact remains that you were instrumental in approving the deployment of SB99 and have made nothing but poor management decisions ever since. *You* are accountable here. What were you thinking?"

"I...," but his voice trailed off. In hindsight he had made a grave error. The original operational strategy was elegant in its simplicity and the subsequent consequences weren't even on the scope. There was a risk that the true identity of the asset would be discovered, but it was negligible. The asset wasn't supposed be in there that long. At least, that was what he had been led to believe. He was starting to regret the trust he'd placed in...

"Well Blake?"

"Well Sir, I was provided with daily highlight reports, none of which raised concern for the welfare of the asset."

"So you're telling us that mission control management was to blame? And choose your words carefully Blake, because bringing this fight to *my* door will not go well for you."

A third voice now entered the fray.

"I don't think you two are fully understanding the implications of this." The others around the table held their tongues. JP wasn't one to get overly involved in discussions. He would observe, ruminate and keep his succinct, and often scathing, responses for the end. But he couldn't stand the nonsense any longer; this was wasting time.

"It is quite simple if you ask me. The political and reputational implications of this... *shit show* are considerably more delicate than any of you can evidently appreciate. We're already in the midst of an internal investigation. As if it's not enough that one of the leading technological minds in our arsenal has been reduced to a quivering wreck because of your incompetence and mismanagement, now I have Whitehall breathing down my neck wanting answers. Answers I am unable to provide without completely destroying any credibility this agency has. I can no longer sit here and listen to your attempts to throw one another under the proverbial bus. Just tell me what we can do about it."

The other attendees looked rather sheepish—each of them wondering whether it was their own head that would roll for this, or that of their neighbour.

"Sir, if I may?" A lighter voice cut through the testosterone-heavy air. Allowance to proceed was given with silence.

"Miss Baxter's progress—" She was interrupted.

"For the sake of the record, please refer to the asset, as 'the asset' going forward."

"Ah, yes, apologies Sir. Since the asset's return, she has undergone extensive psychoanalytic procedures. All standard and advanced measures have been employed, with a view to retain the asset as a viable contributor to the agency. Unfortunately, these measures have failed to sufficiently rehabilitate the asset. And it is my professional opinion that she should not be exposed to high-stress situations. She would likely behave erratically, unpredictably and pose significant risk to the success of any future operation. Her mental instability could compromise any mission outcome. Even if she was desk-bound."

"I see." JP sat pensively a moment. The others dared not speak. He inhaled sharply and deeply, followed by an irritated sigh. He had reflected and now it was time to speak.

"Well dammit, we have a quorum. We'd might as well get on with it. CB do you move to support the decommissioning of SB99?"

"I do, Sir."

"Seconds?"

"I second the motion." Blake didn't raise his gaze from his shabby black leather desk pad. He just wanted this to go away and no longer blemish his own record.

"Any further debate? I'd like to get this wrapped up before my two o'clock."

The others around the mahogany table gave, "Ayes" in agreement.

"The 'ayes' have it. Motion to decommission SB99 passed. Blake, you have an action to arrange for suitable relocation, including a new identity. Throw what you need at it just make it go away. See to it that ties are severed. She never worked for us. Got it?"

Blake nodded.

"Next order of business..."

The meeting continued past two o'clock. SB99 was dutifully actioned. Within a fortnight SB99 was decommissioned, redacted

7

from almost all sources and scarcely given another thought by those on the board. SB99 did not appear on the committee agenda again.

8

At home that night Nicole hoped to devote time and energy to all these notes and messages and get some clarity to her chaotic thoughts. Tonight it wasn't to be: Alfie went to bed as usual but awoke barely an hour into his slumber in a dreadful state. He was sitting bolt upright in bed screaming his little lungs out, utterly inconsolable. He wasn't looking at her properly and it was evident that he wasn't really awake. Flustered, she flicked on the light and tried to soothe him. Calling his name, she tried to get him to wake up. She picked him up from the bed and felt he was soaked with sweat—his Jurassic World pyjamas clinging to his tiny frame. She held him close, his screams giving way to sobs. As he started to calm down she was able to talk to him and managed to pull off his soaked PJs and replace them with clean, dry (although two sizes too small) PAW Patrol ones that he was adamant he'd wear forever.

He nuzzled into her and she sat there on the edge of the bed until he was sound asleep once more. She cautiously shifted him from her lap to the single bed they were sitting on. Adjusting him bit by bit to lay his head onto the now-dry pillow, she managed not to wake him.

She felt strange today. Stranger than she'd felt in a long while. She'd almost forgotten that feeling: uncertainty, unease, ...fear.

8

Although she'd hardly deciphered the clues and messages yet, one thing was evident: these were meant for her. She couldn't very well ignore that, not now.

But what it meant was that someone knew who she was. Or more accurately—who she had been. She felt defeated right now. Maybe it was hormones—they always did take their toll on her. However, since decommission she'd stopped worrying about suppressing the negative feelings they carried to her brain. She'd kept all emotion, negative or otherwise, under wraps for so much of her adult life that she'd forgotten how to feel. The trauma later in life didn't help either, but since her once frequent therapy sessions she'd got a handle on the after-effects of that. When this little pickle came into the world, however, everything changed. Not exactly in the way she would've ever imagined happening but, when all was said and done, she now possessed the most incredible treasure of all and she wasn't going to let anyone jeopardise that.

She knew that these defeatist feelings weren't going to let her analyse the notes and clues in any logical and level-headed way tonight. She was tired. And she just wanted to hold the one thing in her life that loved her unconditionally.

She scooted Alfie over a tad and sandwiched him between her body and the wall, pulled up the duvet, and switched off the lamp. She allowed the darkness to envelop her, listening to all the familiar sounds of the house and the immediate vicinity outside. The rain was pelting the windows—more so at the front of the house than the back—muffling the quieter sounds but providing a good deal of soothing white noise. That, coupled with Alfie's micro-snores, made her eyes heavy with much-needed sleep. She pulled the duvet right up to her chin, pulled closer to Alfie and drifted off into the deepest sleep she'd had in years.

* * *

The next morning she awoke, stiff and achy from the subconscious paralysis experienced by parents not wanting to wake, nor crush, their offspring while they sleep. That, and not wanting to fall out of the single bed. It was a day off for her today. Nothing booked, just a day free to get housework and errands done and then free to collect Alfie from school and have some much-needed Mummy-Alfie time.

She walked home after dropping Alfie off. The school run had been much like any other except Nicole had changed. She was now on alert and frantically scanned each and every face in the playground, looking for someone—anyone—familiar. The day, although cold, was full of bright sunshine. It didn't do anything to lift her mood and paranoia but it did mean she could sport dark sunglasses and not look odd. Helpful, when trying to remain inconspicuous *and* stare at people.

As she walked, she predicted that the laundry would get done, but the bathroom clean wouldn't. She passed a pair of tree surgeons on the roadside dismantling an old Cedar tree that had become diseased. They stepped aside to allow her to pass and she smiled blithely at them—a tremulous nagging paranoia hinting to her that they were plants, here to watch her. She pushed the thought away but quickened her pace nonetheless.

She hastened home and felt relief flood her as she wrenched the door lock into place and turned the key. She slowed her breathing and listened to the silence—only it wasn't silent. She identified and ticked off the usuals: the ticking clock in the living room, the washing machine in full chaotic spin cycle in the kitchen, and a supermarket delivery truck banging its doors a few doors up the street. But also trees... wind... then she felt the cold. She flew from the front door down the hall and into the kitchen. The back door was wide open—the rustling trees outside loud and unmuffled by the double glazing and the cold autumnal wind chilling her face. Or was it the fear?

She paused, listening again. Her back against the wall, she travelled silently and quickly from room to room, clearing each as she moved, needing to satisfy herself that she was alone. She went to the furthest point away from that back door and swept each room in turn. Back downstairs, and content that there was no one hiding, she crossed to the back door and out into the morning sunshine. She searched the back garden for anything disturbed. The back gate was still locked but it was impossible to tell if someone had come in this way. The dry weather over the past few days meant no wet or muddy footprints or indentations in the lawn.

She re-entered the kitchen and slammed the door behind her, turning the key. It was then that she spotted it—an old copy of *Strangers on a Train* by Patricia Highsmith, the haunting chalky faces on the cover art unsettling her stomach. She hesitantly stepped towards the kitchen table and picked up the book. It clearly wasn't a library book. She checked the outside for protruding notes and for folded-down corners—nothing. She opened the front cover; this was a first edition from 1950. The washing machine chimed its ditty-of-completion and the kitchen fell silent except for a low hammering sound. Nicole looked up to identify the source but realised it was coming from her own body. Her heart was hammering hard and sending pulses of blood thudding through her ears.

She took a deep breath and decided she needed a cup of tea.

This was getting out of control. She didn't like it one bit. She had to remind herself that she wasn't just any old single mother though. She was trained for shit like this. She'd experienced a hell of a lot worse. Hell, she'd *done* a lot worse to others.

Get a grip, Nicole.

As the kettle boiled she put her boots out in the hall and hung up her coat. On the next peg hung the tote bag she'd bought three years ago when the local (at the time) town she lived in moved away from plastic carrier bags. A local solicitors firm had had hundreds of these tote bags printed up and were handing them out on the high street. She'd initially refused the freebie but caved on the third offer. The lettering had lasted about a month. She'd used it practically every day since then and it had carried everything from nappies and bottles to shopping and gin. Now it held some loony's threats and clues. Items that were, right now, threatening everything she had worked so fucking hard to protect. *How dare they?* The fear gave way to anger and determination. She lifted the bag off the peg and returned to the kitchen to finish making the tea. The warmness of the kitchen had dissipated out of the open door so she fetched a shawl to wrap around her whilst the heating had a chance to warm the place up again. She settled herself at the small kitchen table and emptied the contents of her bag, laying out everything gathered beside the latest addition to the collection.

She pulled towards her a notepad and pen, neglectfully left on the table a couple of days ago after writing a shopping list, and began to write. She listed out all the clues and where she'd found them. Then beside each one, she wrote down keywords or phrases and tried to organise them in some sort of order.

This done she took a swig of tea—cold.

9

Nicole had spent the last two hours poring over the books and notes that were presented to her and so far she'd come up with only one real certainty.

The person doing this clearly knew who she was and what she was.

The GCHQ Puzzle Book was a little on the nose but it sure as hell got her attention. The book was published a few years ago—the first GCHQ puzzle book to be collated. The Director's Christmas Card had sparked it all off and the idea had really gained traction after some global competition. However, Nicole had already spent years compiling puzzles and brainteasers whenever she was bored. When the bulletin came round asking staff for their contributions, she gladly sent hers in. There was one puzzle she'd concocted where the codebreakers could only solve it by substituting one letter for another. Her dinky letter-swap puzzles had done the rounds on internal email for months before this. When it featured in the puzzle book, it sparked off a social media trend too, with app developers using her algorithm to invent a popular new word game. Still, her original puzzle was included in the book so her name was added to the list of contributors in the back. Obviously, it wasn't her new name, or even the name before that. But it was the name she was known for the longest.

So this person knew her background, at least enough of it to know she worked for GCHQ at one point. They might not necessarily know she contributed to the actual book and had her old name listed in the back. And they might not be aware of her other career attributes.

The other clues were less obvious and there was a certain level of speculation needed here, but things were starting to piece together. She didn't like making these leaps of assumption or guesswork, at least not when you can't then test that theory and act with intelligence. But things were what they were.

Pretty Little Liars was the first clue, hinting at secrets and the threat of those secrets becoming known. Nicole surmised that it could allude to her secrets, or, if the full extent of her secret life was unknown to this person, fit with the other clues that clearly had nothing to do with her.

Quiet Haven - John Grisham
    Retirement home in Clanton - Grisham's famed fictional town
    New staff member - befriends residents and benefits from will, finds malpractice and whistleblows - takes cut. Gets rich, moves on.

Emma - Jane Austen
    p41 - first introduced to Mr Knightley
    Chapter 42 - about Knightley offering Emma to visit Donwell - his home.

Possible connection with Pretty Little Liars: secrets known and threats to tell

Strangers on a Train – obvious deduction > murder someone for someone else therefore no connections made by authorities. Place names important here too perhaps?

Alea iacta est. Latin – The die is cast.

Nicole could see the pieces in front of her. She made some assumptions: the retirement home clue and the *Emma*/Knightley/Donwell clue weren't connected to her. So maybe the *Pretty Little Liars* one was. Which would mean that not only did this person know who she'd been but they clearly knew her secret and, she supposed, wanted to use that as leverage to ... what? *Kill?* From *Strangers on a Train* was she supposed to deduce that the aim was to eliminate someone? And what then, these other clues are to identify that person? Is this person insane?

Nicole struggled to fit a different narrative into all this. This person couldn't seriously expect her to do that? An image of Alfie flashed up into her mind's eye and she couldn't deny it—she'd do anything, anything at all, to keep him safe from harm. But in order to keep him safe, truly safe, she had to keep him with her. She couldn't go gallivanting about murdering people willy-nilly and expect not to get caught. And then what would happen to Alfie? The thought of not being with him was physically painful. Her throat constricted and she felt the arrival of tears burning her eyes and fogging up her vision.

She shook all that aside. She had to keep a clear head.

If she did this, she'd be putting them both at risk. If she was caught... Nicole again shook away the swell of panic and trepidation bubbling up inside her chest.

If she *didn't* do this though, what options did she have? She could move again, access to money would be tricky with not enough time to cover her tracks properly. Not like last time. It'd mean changing their identities again too. Harder this time— Alfie had learnt to spell his name. Is it possible to get a five-year-old to acknowledge a new name and not blurt out the old one? And after all that, it'd be for nothing. No matter where she went, if *he* even knew Alfie was alive it wouldn't matter where they went. You couldn't run and hide from that kind of influence—that kind of power. If *he* initiated a search, they'd be found. And then she'd be apart from Alfie forever. And what would become of him then?

He could say one word and everything she'd worked so hard to build and protect would be shattered. She hadn't appreciated how vulnerable she was until now. She hadn't realised how delicate and precarious all this had turned out to be. She was furious that they held this over her. She was a helpless marionette, unable to look up and see her marionettist.

She was falling. She was being crushed. She felt like a minuscule being stuck under an invisible weight of enormous presence, bearing down on her. She couldn't breathe, she couldn't stand it. It was going to kill her. She needed to stand up, to move. Her eyes were clamped shut and she felt the tears fall unchecked down her cheeks. She sucked in huge lungfuls of air, desperate and faltering.

She had little choice. No one could help her. There was no one to turn to. She was completely alone with no way out. Every dark and twisted, lonely moment of her past flooded her brain and made her feel completely helpless.

No—that was a lie. The emotion lifted as suddenly as it had reared. Like a column of sunshine in the eye of a tornado. For a few, short, precious moments she had clarity. She wasn't helpless.

She possessed all she needed already.

10

The room was small. Hell, the whole flat was small. The living area contained the kitchen, dining room, utility and living room all within thirty square metres. The walls were drab, but clean. The flooring similar. Decor was non-existent: there were no pictures hanging, or plants, or lamps. Just the two overhead bulbs covered with wire and paper shades.

The furniture didn't match and was sparse: a two-seater sofa the only comfortable seating, two wooden chairs, tucked under a spindly Formica table, and a 32" on a simple TV stand under the only window.

The newborn lay on a small crocheted blanket in the middle of that plainly-furnished room. The TV was on. Weekday morning telly; a panel of middle-aged women putting the world to rights. Judging.

The baby was content to watch the colourful shapes moving on screen. The baby's mother anxiously awaited her next health visitor appointment. Laura abhorred these visits. An older woman on the screen was giving her opinion on whether women-only gyms were sexist—Laura considered her opinion typical of a boomer. Then thoughts of her own ageist preconceptions entered her mind. She thought back to her first health visitor appointment. It was a matter of days after she'd first arrived here ready to pop and the woman couldn't have been older than twenty. Her voice had been sickly sweet—Laura heard condescension. And this young girl sat at her table massaging the nipple of a knitted boob to demonstrate self-milking techniques. Laura had baulked.

The door buzzer sounded. Laura crossed from the two-seater sofa and studied the two-inch square blue-tinted screen on the door phone. It wasn't the same woman. Laura didn't bother with platitudes and just buzzed her up.

She glanced across at her newborn, unmoved, as she opened the flat door. She could hear the woman struggling up the stairwell, bags scuffing along the walls and shoes lightly tapping as they met each stair tread. Laura didn't look out though, she just waited by the open door for this woman to materialise within its frame.

"Hello Laura love, how are you today?"

This woman's ease and over-familiarity left an unsavoury taste in Laura's mouth. She'd never so much as spoken to her before.

"Fine thanks."

"My name's Jo." With that, Jo took herself over to the sofa and set her double-wide behind right into its middle. With nowhere else to sit, Laura took to the floor and sat beside her baby.

"How's the little man doing? Have you got your red book? Y'know, your notes?"

Without verbally responding, Laura reached across to the TV stand and picked up the collection of papers stacked there. She'd not so much as read a single word. The pile would gradually get taller with each visit from the midwives. She imagined it'd get taller still with each visit from the health visitors now. She handed them over.

Laura idly watched the TV screen as Jo flicked through the documents and busied herself with peeling labels from one sheet and sticking them onto another.

Jo turned her attention back to Laura and she spent the following hour pointing out all the things Laura was doing wrong, or things she was failing to do at all. Laura couldn't help but feel utter relief that she left just before a nappy change was required. Being scrutinised at times like that didn't help. The midwife watched her last week, to "make sure she was doing it right", and she managed to get shit under three fingernails and up the side of her nose.

Laura closed the door.

She hated this flat. The smells from the takeaway downstairs were already floating up through the communal stairwell. It was probably just coming through the walls. Every day, except Mondays, the smell of aromatic spices would trickle up into her flat. From 3pm until after she'd gone to sleep. She needn't look at her clock at nighttime feeds—she could time them based on the smell. She used to love this smell when it was transient. When it was optional.

She had really been put through the wringer lately. And the feeling of intense paranoia, of being watched, had never left. This flat wasn't hers. She didn't choose it. She didn't want to be here.

But how could she get herself out?

11

She'd been lying here for hours. Anyone observing her would assume she was sound asleep and had been for some time now. But the truth was her mind hadn't switched off yet. The time was maybe two-something. The house was silent. The street was silent, although she did hear a tawny owl about an hour ago. She continued to lie still in the darkness, eyes relaxed and closed, but the sleep just wouldn't come.

Nicole wasn't a stranger to insomnia. She'd gone many a month without proper sleep in the past. If she slept, she'd have the nightmares, so she'd stay awake for as long as she could manage.

Lying here, though, she reckoned she'd just about considered every conceivable possible course of action open to her and every possible subsequent outcome. And she didn't like a single one.

Alfie stirred, banging the wall with his knee as he rolled over. The sudden sound had made her eyes flick open and her heart quicken. She didn't otherwise move. She waited to make sure he was settled before closing her eyes again and tried to think of something else. She tried to just think about mundane, routine things that had happened that day in a now desperate attempt to bore herself to sleep.

She supposed it was inevitable. She'd avoided so many of them so far but now that Alfie was settled and making friends, it was always going to be the case sooner or later. She'd found it when she emptied his book bag earlier—a folded piece of A5 which gave her seriously conflicting emotions. It was wonderful that he'd made friends and that the other kids liked him and wanted him at their parties. She was pleased for that reason, sure. But now she couldn't avoid the social interactions they would inescapably bring with them.

This one was for this coming weekend; an apology from *George's Mummy* for the late notice scrawled along the margin. It was one of those fill-in-the-blanks invites with bright coloured balloons and swirls decorating and framing each blank. This party was to be held at a local soft play centre: *Antz In Your Pantz*. She'd seen it in passing from the car window, secretly hoping Alfie wouldn't observe the garish sign out front by the roadside. They'd managed to avoid it so far. Not any longer it seemed.

What am I going to wear?

The bizarre thought caught her off guard and she actually laughed out loud. She clapped her hand over her mouth to silence herself, alarmed by the sound. What a moronic thing to think about at such a time. What next? Worry about what colour her nails should be painted when she kills someone...

That thought soured her mood again.

She rolled over onto her side and lifted her phone screen towards her face. The motion woke the screen for a couple seconds and she noted the time: 03:18am.

She hated these small hours of the night.

She set the phone back face-down onto the bedside cabinet and rolled back to face the ceiling. From the light seeping

11

around the edges of the curtains, she could clearly see the artex ceiling plaster pattern, looking like a badly drawn map with the topography of mountains and valleys and sticking-up trees. She felt her eyelids get heavy and let them close. Thinking about geography and ox-bow lakes.

Lights out.

12

The day of the party arrived.

Nicole had had to travel into the nearby city earlier in the week just to buy a gift for this George. She could only guess at what the standard thing was to buy for such occasions: not too expensive, not too cheap, nothing which condones excessive violence or anything controversial. There was some dreadful tat in the toy shops—honestly, the choice was pretty crap. After too many minutes, walking up and down the aisles, she'd settled on a two-parter: a small action figure which shot pellets across the room and a promising craft set which was on offer (she bought a second for Alfie, for Christmas), something to do with colour-changing ink.

She'd purchased the card back in town, together with suitably-aged wrapping paper, and had gotten Alfie to write out the card on the kitchen table. His writing was really coming on now and he could sound out and spell anything, so long as the spelling was phonetic, rather than always accurate.

They parked up outside the play centre. Alfie was beside himself, giddy with anticipation. She'd purposefully arrived early and they were sitting in the car for a fair few minutes before others started to arrive. She began recognising some of the other Mums. Alfie was practically yelling into her ear canal every time he spotted a classmate pulling into the car park. She kept him at bay as long as she could. After counting half a dozen attendees, she exited the car immediately followed by Alfie, who had climbed through to the front seat in his haste to get going. He wobbled and lost his balance, plonking his teeny bottom squarely on the steering wheel and setting off the car horn. Well, if she'd wanted a discreet arrival it clearly wasn't to be.

They walked across the car park towards the entrance, the cacophony of sounds gradually getting louder and louder as they approached. Arcade games, neat rows of bowling pins being obliterated, children laughing, yelling, crying. So much noise.

They were greeted at the door by "George's Mummy". *Do these women not have names of their own any more? They become a mere extension of their own offspring?* Nicole pondered this theory of identity a while longer as Alfie patiently waited to be let loose.

The soft play area was a large open-plan, high-ceilinged industrial unit, bolted onto an older brick building from the 1960s or 70s. The older part of the outfit housed a bowling alley and diner. The soft play apparatus dominated the space, as well it should she supposed, and the remaining surround was taken up by as many blue and orange plastic chairs and tables one could hope to cram in. This abundance of furniture, in a space already littered with discarded kids' shoes, meant that there were constant trips and nose-diving infants. These kids were all high on E-numbers and sugar, and were hurtling about at full-pelt, grabbing chairs and barriers to slingshot themselves around corners. It was organised chaos. Well, it was chaos.

Alfie had abandoned Nicole the second he'd been allowed to

and she acknowledged the other Mums from a distance. They were sitting slap bang in the centre of this room—something Nicole had a strong aversion to. She liked a wall at her back so she could take in the whole scene and keep an eye on things. She grabbed herself a pot of tea and a muffin before nabbing a slightly quieter table near the back next to a grabber machine full of weird bog-eyed teddy bears that looked in dire need of rescuing. *Not today chaps, sorry.* She could see the lay of the soft play apparatus well from this vantage point and could easily pick out Alfie in his favourite yellow t-shirt. She smiled and watched him interact with the other kids as she sipped her tea. She was left alone for a good 45 minutes.

Her peripheral vision was alerted to an approaching Mum from the left. She ignored it longer than one would normally but had to cave. She kept her smile fixed on her face and glanced up at the woman now standing behind the next chair.

"Mind if I sit here?"

"No, no, of course not." Nicole tried to answer with as much genteel gentility as she could muster.

"Are you Alfie's Mummy?"

"Yes, I'm Nicole. And you are?" asked Nicole, as she indicated the zoo before her with a wave of her hand.

"Oh I'm Morley's Mummy." *Here we go again!* This time she wasn't going to let it slide.

"What's your name?" she asked. "Morley's Mummy" looked frankly rather startled at being asked if she went by anything other than "Morley's Mummy". It took her a second to absorb the request but she smiled and replied, "Tasha". *See, that wasn't so hard.*

The pair sat discussing the attitudes of the teacher, the phonics progress, how tall the boys were compared to some of

12

the younger ones, the deluge of emails that emanated from the school office every week. All very convivial and going swimmingly. Nicole was almost enjoying herself, when Morley arrived at the table demanding something to eat from his mother. She looked slightly ashamed but didn't deny the boy his request. She pulled a large sharing bag of Monster Munch from her rucksack and handed it over. Without a single word of thanks, he was off at top speed disappearing into the jungle of roped walls and padded shapes. Nicole got a glimpse of yellow and followed it along as Alfie's full form appeared at the topmost level. He waved down to her with a massive grin on his face.

She glanced up at the humongous clock hanging on the side wall—they'd sat there for almost a whole hour! She turned back to Tasha and checked if she was okay keeping an eye out for Alfie whilst she popped to the toilet. The party was winding up soon and she wanted to be ready to head home as soon as she could. She'd normally have called Alfie over to go with her but he was buried so deep she didn't suppose she could fetch him out quickly—and she really needed a wee.

Tasha was, of course, fine with acting as lookout. Nicole saw another blur of yellow just as the door closed, muffling the sounds and making her ears ring.

She'd only been three minutes. She re-entered the area to find the parents associated with George's party all standing and mingling about, clearly getting ready to vacate the premises. George was dutifully handing out bright blue paper party bags to his guests, as his mother kept him restocked from a wicker basket she held.

Nicole approached, expecting to see Alfie in the melee. No yellow. She looked up towards the play area expectantly—

nothing.

Tasha appeared at her side. "It was nice meeting you Nicole."

"You too Tasha. Um, have you seen Alfie?"

"Oh, he got his party bag and started out to your car with your Mum."

"My m...," she stopped breathing. Her mouth just gaped at Tasha. Tasha could clearly sense something wrong and started to try and explain, evidently worried that this had happened on her watch. "But she said...," her voice trailed off.

Nicole wasn't listening anyway. She pushed past her and her horrible sprog and made for the exit. Breaking into a run—a sprint—she bowled through a pair of older boys at the doorway. She didn't hear the insults they tossed her way. She wouldn't have given a shit even if she had. She flew out into the car park and came to a halt, frantically searching the car park with her keen eyes.

"Mummy I thought I'd lost you," came the most wonderful sound she'd ever heard in her entire life. Alfie was standing right next to her beside the building. She'd run right past him. He just stood there on his own. Now, he was bawling from the relief. And so was she. She collapsed onto her knees, the wet tarmac seeping into her jeans, and held him close.

Tasha had, considerably more slowly, followed her out. She was carrying Alfie's jumper and Nicole's jacket and brought them over. Nicole looked up and half-heartedly thanked her, realising that they were both trembling. Tasha made her exit, feeling guilty and perhaps a tad awkward. She had little more to add to her previous statement: she thought the older woman she saw was his Nan and gave an embarrassed shrug.

Alfie was so upset Nicole couldn't get him to say much at all. She carried him to the car and got him all strapped in. It was only then she noticed he was holding something else. She'd earlier assumed that it was the party bag, but she had that in her own hand now. The light had faded already at this hour and the sodium lighting was giving everything a dim orange tint.

"She gave it to me," said Alfie.

"Who sweetheart? George's Mummy? Morley's Mummy?" *Christ, I am doing it now.*

"I don't know," he said, and he handed it to her. It was a book. A book far too thick for his reading level and brightly adorned in scribbles and doodles. Nicole took the book and moved it nearer the open car door. It was a book called *Tom Gates - Top of the Class (nearly)* by Liz Pichon. There was a slip of paper poking out of the top.

Nicole looked at Alfie. His tear-reddened eyes looked back at her as if waiting for something. She tried to smile and put him at ease. He tentatively smiled back and asked for his party bag. He wanted to know what colour balloon he'd been given.

Nicole closed the back door and moved to open the driver's door—all the while staring at the book in her hands.

Fucking bitch! I get the message.

13

The drive home was quiet. The anxiety and tears that had followed the ordeal had wiped Alfie out and he was subdued in the back seat. The radio was on—some droney voice muttering about austerity and interest rates. Nicole's mind was racing. She was fuming. Furious and savage thoughts flooded through her brain—all the ways she wanted to hurt that woman. To rob her of her life, for even daring to threaten her boy. *Who the fuck does she think she is?*

However, at least now she knew it was a *she*. That practically halved the pool of potentials. And she was older. Old enough to pass as Alfie's grandmother. That narrowed the field even more. So all Nicole needed to do was find a female aged early sixties or older, in a town full of retired old women. *Marvellous.*

Nicole was so enraged and distracted she flew right past the left turn that would cut off the corner and bring her out near The Old Mill on the south side of town—the wider road and faster route. The unfamiliar surroundings brought her mind out of its murderous reverie and she took her foot off the accelerator. She leant forward over the steering wheel in an effort to get a better view of the road sign up ahead. The headlights hit the faded wooden post.

Right... Millbrook two, Dunwell a quarter straight ahead...and beyond that will be Lower Hobham, then home.

Nicole ignored her urge to turn around to take her usual route and carried on straight towards Dunwell. Dunwell was a small village borne from the convergence of three small roads. There was a small grassy hillock where these roads met and a proud village sign with DUNWELL in carved wooden letters, although the "U" had slightly rotted away. Above the name was a rather peculiar depiction of a farmer standing beside an old well. And a sheep. In the momentary illumination from the passing headlights, it looked to Nicole as if the farmer was shoving the sheep into the well. Beside this village sign sat a dilapidated bench and a red phone box. The only other contents of this village were a few small, slightly unkempt cottages and a tiny corner shop. She continued northwards—mostly fields out this way.

She entered Twynesham from the west. The western side of town was dominated by agricultural farmland, mostly owned and tended by the Midrake family. Nicole had overheard some juicy gossip in the library a while back during an embroidery workshop. The Midrake family lived out Millbrook way. They farmed intensively and efficiently, turning over a decent profit and putting some of that profit back into community programmes and schemes to benefit the whole town. As such, they were well regarded.

They had a notorious rivalry with the Lock family who had land that dominated the eastern side of town. There was some dispute over land ownership between the heads of the families a couple of generations back and it lingered today—despite no one remembering the details. The gossip she'd heard was Ol' Bob Midrake being in the local, The Bluebell, when the younger son of his old foe stumbled in, already worse for wear. There was some sort of fracas and words were exchanged. It sounded to Nicole as though the Midrakes were wanting to buy up the Lock land on the cheap before this chap and his brother died leaving it intestate. So the younger Lock was more than a little disgruntled at the notion, loudly exclaiming that he'd rather it went to ruin and that he'd burn the place down first. Despite the age-gap, it sounded as though the gossiping women were certain the younger Lock would die before the older Midrake.

Anyway, enough of town politics, it was time for Alfie to get to bed and for Nicole to wrap her head around these clues once and for all. She needed to piece this thing together fast and work out her exit strategy.

She might have blindly followed orders in the past but those days were long gone. There was no way she was just going to take this random quack's word for it—she was going to do her own recon and then decide what to do. It might buy her some time to identify a way out of all this before the point of no return.

Could she be so lucky?

* * *

Later that evening, with Alfie tucked up sound asleep and grasping the limp balloon carcass in his hand (it popped between car and house), Nicole settled back at the kitchen table with her notebook and the stack of books. She'd placed the latest addition to the collection beside the others and sat back to take it all in.

What a random collection of novels. Her analyst brain told her that the chances of direct links between them all was negligible. She re-read her notes:

    Quiet Haven – John Grisham
    Retirement home in Clanton – Grisham's famed fictional town
    New staff member – befriends residents and benefits from will, finds malpractice and whistleblows – takes cut. Gets rich, moves on.

    Emma – Jane Austen
    p41 – first introduced to Mr Knightley
    Chapter 42 – about Knightley offering Emma to visit Donwell – his home.

    Possible connection with Pretty Little Liars: secrets known and threats to tell
    Strangers on a Train – obvious deduction > murder someone for someone else therefore no connections made by authorities. Place names important here too perhaps?

    Alea iacta est. Latin – The die is cast.

And then added below:

    Tom Gates – Top of the Class by Liz Pichon

She had no prior knowledge or understanding of Tom Gates, other than there were quite a lot of them in the Young Readers section in the library and that they were very popular and very colourful. She could see Alfie reading books like these in a couple of years' time. She opened the book at the page marked with the scrap of paper. It was right at the start. There was nothing on the paper at all. She read the first page: it was a poster for the school elections. Nothing of any particular note other than the school name—Oakfield—and the fact there were elections. *Oh please let this not be a politician.* She jotted these down on her pad.

She returned back to the first clue—the short story by John Grisham. She opened up her laptop and started to click away at the soft touch keys. She always loved sitting in the near-darkness with just the light from the screen and the backlit keys. It took her back. She tap-tapped away and read all she could about the places, people and names mentioned in the text, jotting them all down and filing them away for later.

Next, she picked up the copy of *Emma*. She read page forty-one, then that whole chapter. Then she re-read Chapter forty-two. And then the scrap of paper. She was sure this was connected to Knightley and maybe therefore his residence Donwell. But there are so many names and places mentioned by Jane Austen, maybe it was Suckling, Highbury or Churchill or Weston or Elton and Box Hill.

She moved the open *Emma* to one side and picked up *Strangers on a Train*. The cover still made her feel uneasy. She slammed it face down onto the tabletop and huffed. Her back hurt.

She got up to stretch and started to make herself a cup of tea. As the kettle got louder, the white noise of it actually offered respite and soothed her head. Up until that point, she hadn't truly appreciated how many noises were crying out inside her mind. She allowed the disturbance to wash over her and listened to nothing but the jet-engine kettle and the rumbling, bubbling as the water inside reached temperature. She told herself that when the noise ceased, the thoughts would

13

be settled, the pieces still and cooperative. The click of the kettle switch signalled it was time. Time to make tea. And time to concentrate.

The muddled overlapping thoughts were calmed and she approached each potential puzzle piece anew. Acknowledging that she wasn't expecting them to all fit was helping, it took the pressure off.

She picked up the GCHQ puzzle book. The only book that she'd essentially discarded, assuming it to just be the vessel for informing her that she was identified. But maybe it was something more. She idly flicked through the pages and then spotted something—that piece of paper. She'd forgotten there was a piece of paper. It had nothing written on it, although it was placed neatly at page 87, just where she'd found it. Page 87... the page with her most popular puzzle on it. This couldn't be a coincidence. She looked down at the familiar puzzle.

And then it dawned on her. *Moron—of course!*

Her mind was suddenly alert and her fingers were typing at a ferocious rate. She was a dozen lines into the code already, her tea forgotten about. The code she wrote with such ease and fluency would pull in all the keywords and text from the books and passages she'd been steered towards, as well as every permutation of those words with one letter altered. She would then programme in all the place names from here in a ten-mile radius for now (she could always extend it later) and also the census and electoral roll data for all residents in that same area.

She was on a roll. Hell, she might as well tap into Experian data warehouses and mine that data source too. If she could connect up people and behaviours as well as flat data such as place names, then she could really propel this whole search thing forward.

Again and again, she pulled in complex datasets and applied an algorithm to change each letter and pull all of *that* together in an ever-expanding data lake where she would then write even more code to cross-reference millions of data points against a million others and see what hits she got. This was going to take some time, as well as a significant amount of hacking, to get the full, unfiltered details—but she felt kind of invigorated. She found herself smiling a little bit. This part of her brain had been dormant for so long and now she felt alive, her fingers flashing over the keys, her rumbling tummy going unfed and ignored.

The minutes becoming hours.

14

It had taken a few hours to get the data mining done. Whilst she'd waited for the data to download, she'd written and implemented an inspiringly brilliant WiFi sniffer program that piggybacked on all the nearest connections, flitting from one to another, breaking through the encryption protocols and essentially hopping on and hopping off every few gigs. The program routed these connections through multiple overseas IP addresses whilst she was at it. This way she could not only spread the download to maximise speed but she could also minimise the likelihood of ever being traced. In the highly improbable event that the systems administrators at all these organisations she was hacking into even spotted the trace elements of code she'd left behind, they'd have difficulty in tracing it back to the UK, let alone middling, inconsequential Twynesham.

She'd left her programs running and taken herself off to bed around 12:30am. Considerably earlier than she'd hoped—the sniffer had worked faster than she'd expected—seems that older people in rural settings really don't bother too much with data security and higher-level encryption. Luddites.

She slept like a baby that night, as in she woke every couple hours because she was starving. After the third such interruption from her gut, she resigned herself to another day of feeling bloody exhausted. It took her a minute to recall which day of the week it was—Tuesday. *School day. Work at 10 am.* Nicole groaned and rolled over, burying her face in the cold side of her pillow. Alfie suddenly burst through the bedroom door and performed a flying mantis martial arts body slam right into her, his knee connecting perfectly with her left kidney. He, naturally, thought this outcome was hysterical. She had to admit defeat—the only recourse now was a prolonged and unrelenting ticklefest. Her mood lifted.

The pair got themselves dressed and headed down for breakfast. Nicole wouldn't normally let Alfie watch cartoons as it usually resulted in his eating speed dramatically decreasing, but they were up unusually early and she needed him to be distracted. Rice Krispies were the order of the day—for them both. She ate with her bowl cradled under her chin; she'd never been able to eat cereal without dribbling it every other mouthful. She hoped she wasn't the only adult to suffer such indignities and took a seat in front of her dormant laptop and tapped the spacebar.

The screen awoke and displayed a completion summary— just as she'd drafted it last night. Although now her programs had populated the information to demonstrate how it had mined just shy of 89 million data points and had found 1,828 possible matches given the parameters in the code. *This isn't too bad.* She'd expected more.

She opened the list of results to review manually and see what trends she could spot—sometimes these things were just better done with human eyes. The majority of person-related hits were, of course, concentrated in and around the city of Blyworth, ten miles or so to the southwest. Her instincts told her to disregard those; this felt more Midsomer than Sherlock. She adjusted the parameters and refined the results: 251. This was now focussed on Twynesham and a four-mile radius from the library's coordinates. She had to centre it somewhere.

She scanned the list to see whether anything leapt out at her. *Too many long shots still in here.* She revisited the code again, this time applying weighting to the results dependent on how many of her book titles, references and notes matched. This then spat out categorised lists and she could focus on the most likely candidates first.

The remixed theme tune to Postman Pat wafted across the table. She looked up from her screen and watched along with Alfie for a few minutes—he didn't notice. In this escapade, Pat had taken receipt of a new hat for Mrs Goggins and instead of keeping it safely in the box, had systematically shared the hat with Ajay, Dr Gilbertson and Ted Glen. One used it as a Frisbee to attempt to knock their own hat loose from a tree. It failed and Pat resorted to retrieving them both with his helicopter. *Honestly, how this man doesn't get fired is beyond me.*

Her list was shortening. She left Pat to his one delivery of the day—lamenting the ease of his quiet rural life—and turned her attention back to the screen, digging into the top five.

The top result was Geoffrey "Donny" Dondell. He was in his early eighties and had lived in the same house since birth. His father, Ernest, had inherited the house from his tenant farmer father. Geoffrey's wife had died some 18 years prior. He had strong church connections and one daughter.

Next on the list was a teenager called Harry Steven Slanton. Some digging satisfied Nicole's curiosity as to why the teen's parents weren't also named in this list. Harry was currently living with a foster family just outside town. He attended the school just up the road; athletic kid, good grades. The word "Oak" connected to him also. It was in the title of a poem he wrote that had won a competition and been published.

Third was a dog-groomer called Angela Airsdale. She owned and ran the Doggie Spa on the high street. Her maiden name had been Dondell. Ah, she was Geoffrey's daughter. In her late fifties, married to Julian Airsdale.

Next up was a middle-aged female called Tracey Elaine Wolston. She lived in Maple Gardens—a collection of 60s bungalows built on a parcel of land the church sold off. She was late forties, single, no kids, full-time employment at a care home called Clandon Respite Care and Nursing Home just outside the village of Dunwell.

Last in Nicole's top five results was Jennifer Ella Watkins. She lived in Dunwell village and her mother's maiden name was Cladton. Late 30s, primary school teacher in Falke and currently 29 weeks pregnant with her first child.

Apart from that poem, there were no obvious links to Oakfield or politicians/elections in this top five. But these five felt worth exploring. The next results down seemed even more tenuous than these. And Nicole felt reluctant to move over these five just yet. More work was needed here.

Postman Pat had finished for the day. Nicole was just getting started.

* * *

Later that afternoon, after a busy but uneventful day at the library, Nicole walked home with Alfie. They took the longer route through town rather than cutting through the dark alleyways that connected up the lokes and closes and cul-de-sacs that criss-crossed between the collections of cottages and new builds that sprawled outwards from the middle of town. Alfie stopped to look in at the bakery window, eyeing up a shortbread cookie with a smiley face drawn on the front in shoddily piped icing. At that precise moment Nicole's attention was redirected to the window of the shop next door. Well, if you can call an estate agents a "shop"—Nicole always considered them with a fair amount of disdain.

There were quite a few estate agents in town but this one, Dewfuss & Hassell, was the more high-brow offering and therefore the least visited by locals. Only the very wealthy, second-home buyers seemed to frequent this establishment. Dominating the window and obscuring the plush, decadent furnishings inside, were a select few of the properties currently on their books—or at least recently purchased, as some had those small triangular corner adornments signifying *Under Offer* or *SSTC. Just an excuse for the agents to humbly brag about how effective they are at selling,* thought Nicole.

These six panels were all illuminated by hidden, soft white LEDs and all showcased large, palatial properties. Not one of them was below £800,000 and as such, they all sported grandiose and promising names ending in *Lodge, Manor* or *Farm*. The images beside the latter clearly depicted buildings that hadn't seen the backside of a sheep in decades. They were all immaculate and boasted of rooms no one knew they even needed. *Just the sort of property "Oakfield" might suit.*

Her distracted mind was a pushover for Alfie and they walked the remainder of the way home with him munching on his cookie and Nicole eager to do some research. She hadn't considered online listings yet—how stupid of her. Especially seeing as these listing sites also kept records of historical purchases.

She wrote the code in her head as they walked and Alfie babbled about school and what he had for lunch. He was most disappointed at the lack of ketchup available for his hot dog.

Alfie stopped dead in his tracks. She took a step more before realising and turned to face him.

"What's wrong little man?"

"Mummy, where is my family?"

Nicole's stomach plummeted. She wasn't sure how to best respond to this. She knew it'd likely crop up sooner or later but she still hadn't decided on an official line she was happy with.

"Well, pickle, *I* am your family—you are *my* family." She crouched down beside him so their eyes were level. "Some families are big, some small. What makes a family *a family* is love. And if you have love then that's all you need, eh?"

He eyed her, unconvinced, but didn't say anything.

"It's unfortunate that my mummy and daddy aren't around any more but I promise I'll always be here for you little pickle... to give you cuddles and kisses... and tickles," she smiled at him as she saw his face break into a grin. "I love you very much little pickle."

"I love you too, Mummy." They gave each other a big squeeze.

"Let's get home eh? What do you fancy for dinner?"

"Beans."

"Daft question. Come on, let's get going, it's getting chilly." She took his hand in hers and they crossed the road to dive into a cut-through. She felt a tear roll down her cheek. *It's the cold* she thought, although she wasn't completely convinced.

15

The evening was spent in two parts: first was dinner, bath time, story time and bedtime; the second was coding, searches and revelations.

She started with a simple search of the three leading listing sites. She narrowed the search parameters, looking for only Freehold properties in the immediate area of Twynesham and took a punt on price parameters. The results were extremely interesting. There was a property, just outside the core of the town, to the east. Its name was Oakfield Farm. The HM Land Registry provided the rest:

Detached. Freehold. Sold three times since 1997. First for £149,000, then again in 2003 for £289,000 and last month for £767,000.

Woah.

She clicked on the small thumbnail and swiped through dozens of photographs showing an immaculate property: 5 beds, 3 baths... 4000 sq ft in 0.9 acres. There were floorplans too and an official property boundary map showing the exact location—including all entry points and vulnerabilities.

Nicole opened a second window and within seconds was hacking into the servers of Dewfuss & Hassell. They were named as the most recent agent to sell this property—their fancy script-font logo instantly recognisable at the side of the entry.

She was in.

She easily found the records for Oakfield Farm and could browse through dozens of pages of correspondence and file notes. The sellers were the son and daughter, acting with Power of Attorney on behalf of an elderly lady who had lived there with her late husband. There had been a lot of back and forth between a Mrs Tracey Wolston (*my number four!*) and the family's solicitor. She clearly had designs on this property and it also appeared that she knew about its market appearance ahead of schedule, as the first correspondence was direct from her to the agents asking to make an offer before it went on the market. The original asking price was in excess of £850,000 but she'd somehow bartered them down. Not only that, she appeared to not have a mortgage offer—as in, she didn't need one. Noted as a cash buyer, although someone in the agent's office had annotated the scanned document with a large question mark.

The sale appeared to be proceeding; contracts had been exchanged and completion was imminent. With no onward chain, the matter seemed all but settled.

The documents also revealed Tracey Wolston and an Elaine Wolston had been making offers on similarly priced properties in neighbouring villages, but they had all been outbid or unaccepted. These were all in the last eight to nine months.

The name of Tracey (and Elaine's) solicitor was cited multiple times: an independent named Gerald J. Jarvis. He had a registered office address in Falke, about four miles north of Twynesham towards the coast. Falke was fancy and Nicole rarely spent time there, feeling too conspicuous and low-class to grace its streets. Sure she could fit in should she wish to, but it would mean buying red trousers and Hunter wellies. She didn't have the energy to keep up the pretence.

She tried to find a way into the records and files of this Gerald J. Jarvis but he, rather incredulously, had no online presence at all. Either this guy was so advanced he had a completely locked-down personal server with impenetrable firewalls, or he used pen and paper. The latter was more likely. This would test her field agent capabilities. She'd hope she wouldn't need to get her hands dirty—well, *physically* dirty.

She sat back to take stock of the information she'd uncovered and concluded that she had sufficient evidence to pursue the Tracey Elaine Wolston line of enquiry and see where it would lead. She opened her notebook to a fresh page and began to jot down the key pieces of information she had learned, along with some questions or observations of her own:

Managing director of care home – average salary? How can afford cash buy 767K?
Esp on single income.
Gerald J. Jarvis – Falke. Paper file – possible to obtain? Is it even required?
Vulnerabilities: Large new home, secluded and unfamiliar
Loner – no immediate family members
Check: Medical history/weaknesses
Known associates
Work premises/vulnerabilities
Income – exploit?

The most important question wasn't worth scribbling down. She didn't need to be reminded of it and it had no answer. Why this woman should be marked for death she couldn't fathom. Nicole had contextual information at her fingertips, but the *reasons* and *motives* were always harder to find. Far less likely to be found in hard data, these things were nuanced and undocumented now. She'd have to begin her own one-woman reconnaissance operation. In the past, this legwork had always been carried out by a team of trained professionals who would spend weeks, months even, compiling and recording every purchase, interaction and connection the mark made.

Nicole was going it alone with only her own smarts to get her through. She tried to recall all that her training had taught her. She was more nervous about this part than any other. It was this part of her training that had so spectacularly failed her on her last operation. She reminded herself that the likelihood of Tracey Wolston noticing her surveillance at all, let alone brutally torturing and assaulting her, was highly improbable.

She would still need to second guess every move she made and cover her tracks extremely well if she was going to pull this off. She would take her time, blackmailer willing.

No one was going to get the better of her this time.

16

She'd already become used to calling him Alfie now. His old name was now only used when she talked about him to others. She bundled the toddler up against the winter air and strapped him into the pushchair, zipping him up into the plush seat liner, safe from the world in that cocoon. He fell back asleep almost immediately, his obscenely long, thick eyelashes rested on his puffed-up cheeks.

Laura gathered up her holdall and slipped the strap over her head. The pushchair was already heavily leaden with toddler-related paraphernalia and her assessment determined one more bulky bag would send Alfie skyward.

She navigated the pushchair through the doorway and let the door shut behind her. She didn't need a last look. Besides, it was very early and they had a very long way to go. She didn't need to be getting all sentimental. Especially not about that place.

The first destination was Stevenage Bus Station, Stop K. They had three buses to navigate before they even reached Cambridge. It was going to be a terribly long day.

* * *

Laura burdened herself with her holdall for one last march. The National Express had taken them as far as Blyworth and she had followed a very convoluted route through rural Norfolk to arrive at her final destination—Twynesham.

She'd never been here before. Buying a house without viewing it first would be considered unorthodox by some—bloody nuts by others. But here they were. The house was a tiny, end-terrace with grey flint walls and white brick accents. The iron gate hung open on one hinge and the green wheelie bin was missing, but she was in love. The frontage was illuminated by a solitary streetlamp. The road was quiet. She looked at the windows of the house next door. Through a crack in the curtain, she could make out a head bobbing about against the light of the TV. There was no one to witness their arrival. No one asking questions. She could be anyone she wanted to be—she chose Nicole.

Here they were home. At last.

Safe from prying eyes, reviews and check-ups—and scrutiny.

Safe. From them. From him.

Home.

17

The following week was spent sandwiching in being a parent between shifts at the library and following Tracey around town. At the weekend she'd taken Alfie out for a drive in the car. She wanted to get a feel for the journey, noting timings, residences and businesses she'd need to pass and what CCTV and security they had in place. It was remarkably easy to find an unmonitored route between her own home, Tracey's current abode, her soon-to-be new home of Oakfield Farm, and Clandon House—her workplace just outside Dunwell village.

Alfie was good as gold, sitting in the back listening to the radio and playing eye-spy out of the window.

Clandon House, or to give it its full title: Clandon Respite Care & Nursing Home, was an old manor house that had been converted sometime in the 1980s into a care facility. It was a long, narrow house, with all the bedrooms facing the large, sun-drenched gardens and the north-facing windows lining a long, cold and draughty dark hallway. The floorplans were a cinch to find in the recently digitised planning archive on the local authority website. They were immensely helpful. She could consider the layout of the site with ease and paired with aerial photographs from the web she could also gauge the ingress points and places around the grounds with the most promising vantage positions.

She could also see the most likely locations for the administrative offices and how she'd best approach them. She needed to understand more about the set-up within but really didn't want the exposure of visiting the place. It might well have been easy to ask for a tour under some guise of being the relative of a prospective resident, but she'd really prefer to keep her face and name—false as it would be—out of the picture altogether.

By the end of the third week, she had established Tracey's schedule, and it was mundane. She lived alone, would leave for work around 9:30 am and travel by car direct to Dunwell, taking approximately 12 minutes if there were no tractors en route. She shopped weekly in town and had regular appointments at a small, independent beauty salon off the market square. She didn't seem to date or go out with friends. Her phone traffic was limited to work-related calls and messages.

Clandon House was where she spent most of her time. She would enter the building using a converted full-height window almost directly into her office, and from Nicole's vantage point she was able to monitor movement around the building from the north. The plans suggested there were no interconnecting doors operational since the refurbishment, so all movement was via this hallway running the length of the property. Nicole observed that Tracey rarely left her spacious office—once belonging to Lady Hutton as her Morning Room—and those who visited her never stayed for long.

Nicole had spent evenings reading the inspection reports for the facility on the CQC website. The Care Quality Commission, she found, was an independent regulator who inspected all such facilities throughout the UK, and all their reports were available online. Clandon was overall rated *Outstanding*, with a couple of

Good ratings under the *Effective* and *Responsive* categories.

Well-led was rated as *Outstanding*—which given what Nicole had witnessed only the previous week, seemed far-fetched. The inspection was only conducted last year; it seemed unlikely that things had gone downhill that fast. Nicole speculated that the most probable explanation was that Tracey was pulling the wool over someone's eyes, somewhere. From her vantage point—which was as brilliant a vantage point as one could hope for—Nicole could see so much already.

She'd found this spot on her first recce. A narrow farmers' track circumnavigated the boundary of Clandon House and butted up against a high flint wall—an original 18th Century feature. The overgrown gardens of the house beyond this wall completely obscured it, and the grounds beyond it, for about 25 metres. There were no gardeners on the books since austerity cuts in the early noughties so old piles of dead wood and leaves were now mulch. Nicole assessed the loke well before deciding that this was a safe bet; the farmland this side of Dunwell had been left to fallow and was not due to be touched again for a while. This track didn't appear to be used by anyone else, perhaps the odd dog-walker or horse-rider, but then Dunwell Woods offered much nicer surroundings for such endeavours and she'd not witnessed any dog or horse tracks yet. The hedgerow on the farm side of the track was overgrown too, disguising her car from any wandering eyes.

Nicole parked in the loke, blocking it, and used a fallen oak trunk to scale the high wall. Once at the top, she was able to walk down the other side. Waste leaves, cuttings and old branches had evidently been piled up against the wall for many years prior, creating a convenient ramp. She'd found the ideal crouching place behind two brown, dead Christmas trees dumped behind some azalea bushes. It was from here that she could view the entirety of the estate from the rear, including the hexagonal Morning Room with its abundance of windows on her far left and the long dark rear hallway stretching out to the right.

The tall, multi-paned windows were equally spaced along this back wall and coincided with each of the front-facing rooms' doorways—both ground floor and first floor. As these windows were positioned at knee-height up, Nicole had an unencumbered view in. Beside each doorway was a plastic frame where the room number and occupant's name was placed, as well as some text that was too small to read from this distance. Beside that, was a small light bulb—the small ridged sort you'd likely find on a submarine console. This light changed colour to signify calls from the occupant, calls for assistance by staff and others like that. Nicole gathered that a red light meant that a staff member needed help from another, as invariably someone came running when a red light went on. Amber lights were evidently assigned to the call button for the occupant—these were ignored most of the time. Green was the default OK signal. Green lights were rare.

Residents did not appear to mingle or move around on their own, despite the fact that the CQC report suggested that they could—and did. Nicole had witnessed many rooms being locked when staff walked back out into the hall.

All the while, Tracey Wolston would sit her ample bottom in a wing-backed chair and flit between her phone screen, her iPad screen or a woman's magazine. She had her own coffee machine in her office and an endless supply of biscuits from a large dark-blue tin that sat on a table at her right elbow. Tracey seemed content to exist in this hexagonal bubble—unnoticed and undisturbed for hours at a time.

Every so often Nicole would observe her struggle up from her armchair and cross to the large mahogany desk. Her legs appeared stiff and she hobbled a bit. She would unlock and open the left side bottom drawer and remove a metal tin—like the sort you'd keep petty cash in, with a handle on top. This appeared to be a stash of medication—a stash that wasn't kept under lock and key, and recorded, as with the large cabinet at the back of the room. Nicole had witnessed this cabinet being opened multiple times in the few occasions she'd sat here behind the azaleas. Most of the time it was by Tracey, but sometimes by the staff. So evidently this was where some, if not all, the medicines were being kept. A collection of loose paper sat on the cabinet's top, secured onto a wooden clipboard.

Nicole had twice witnessed Tracey—always later in the day—take this clipboard of paper over to her desk. She would appear to remove the top sheet and after some scribbling, replace it with another from her desk. The one removed would be fed to the shredder that sat beside her. Tracey would return the clipboard to its normal position and then open the cabinet and remove a box or bag of something or other and invariably drop it into her large, hideous handbag.

* * *

On the third of such visits to the grounds of Clandon House, Nicole decided that she'd seen enough. As she began to extricate herself from her vantage point, she heard the unmistakable sound of a horse's whinny. Her head swivelled around to face the direction it came from. She caught sight of the back ends of two horses as they passed a disused wrought iron gate to her right. She knew that, heading the way they were, they would turn a couple of bends to the left and come up directly behind her trusty black hatchback, blocking the loke.

Nicole sprang up from her position and ran as fast as she could whilst keeping as crouched as possible. She powered up the earthy slope and chanced a look. She could see the very tops of two riders' hats—one black, one navy—side by side and nearing the second bend. Without missing a beat, she vaulted over the flint wall and landed six feet below, beside her passenger door. Hand already in her pocket, she depressed the unlock button on the key fob. The lights blinked in recognition and she heard the familiar clunk of mechanisms shifting within. She jogged around to the opposite side, looking again up towards the approaching riders, and watched as the horses' heads rounded the bend together. She flicked up her hood and lowered her head, hands trembling as she grabbed for the door. Wrenching it open, she landed heavily in the driver's seat. She was fully aware of both horses and riders now bearing down on her in the loke. She could hear their conversation trail off as they observed her car and voiced their annoyance of the obstruction and, "...down-right cheek!" She slammed her door and, without any acknowledgement or apology, started the engine, rammed it into gear and released the handbrake. Her rising apprehension made her rev harder than she needed to, terrified she'd stall. But the clutch held and the sudden burst of acceleration pushed her back into the seat. The resulting exhaust and dust caused the horses to rear up and the riders to shout, their irritation turned to anger—but she couldn't hear them now.

She was out of there. She knew the route the track took very well by now but she'd refrained from taking the sharp bends at

17

any measure of speed before. The right-angled turns, tracing the outline of the field, were pretty unforgiving and, after the second of such bends, she slowed to a more manageable speed. She hoped the riders wouldn't bother chasing her down. There was a sharp turn through a tractor-gap in the hedgerow coming up and this took her out onto the road to Millbrook. She took the turn, looking round to make sure she wasn't followed, and joined the road.

At least she needn't go back again. There was nothing left to see here. Her attention would be better suited back behind her screen.

She was safe behind her screen.

18

On reflection she'd done the right thing. She was angry at herself for getting in that position but when she thought back on it, she had done the right thing. She'd been bloody lucky, but it had been worth it. They hadn't seen her jump the wall, or seen her face.

She now knew that Tracey Wolston was a poor manager and was up to something involving the drugs and medication meant for those under her care. She was an overweight woman—actually, heavier than that, more obese. And her abundance of naff jewellery, caked-on make-up and immaculate false nails suggested she never did a hard day's work.

Her lopsided walk and her thieving of meds hinted at an ailment, or two. And this was definitely an area Nicole needed to explore—and exploit.

She spent that evening hacking through the firewalls of all three doctors' surgeries in town. Typical, Tracey wasn't a registered patient of the first two—the most likely candidates. Instead, Tracey, for whatever reason, had registered herself with the smallest surgery, with just one registered GP. And her medical records made for some interesting reading.

Tracey Elaine Wolston was 48 and had lived in town all her life. She was born with a congenital heart defect—an aortic valve stenosis—which didn't sound good. When she was a child she'd had a mechanical valve put in and a subsequent replacement twenty-odd years later. As such, she had to take regular medication to keep her blood thin—an anticoagulant called Warfarin. She was also edging closer to being diagnosed with diabetes and had had a few tests and consultations listed about that. Most recently, she had been complaining of joint pain and swelling. The Doc noted perimenopausal and advised over-the-counter ibuprofen and paracetamol. Most interesting though, was a severe egg allergy.

Now this is promising...

Only a fortnight ago Nicole had received an email from the school about the free flu vaccinations they were offering to all children. She had dutifully clicked the link and filled in the form for Alfie to get his. One of the questions that had stood out was whether or not he had an allergy to egg protein. This had struck an odd chord with Nicole, flashing up images in her mind's eye of diseased chicken feet and undercooked egg whites. There was a note on Tracey's 'Patient alerts and reminders' section confirming her eligibility for annual free flu jabs.

Nicole scrolled through the notes and within seconds she was viewing all previous vaccination dates when Tracey had taken advantage of the offer. She hadn't missed a single year. Every one since 2017 had been administered by the same local pharmacist and all within the same two-week window—the first two weeks of November.

She had time.

* * *

Nicole hadn't performed any real-time hacking in years. She hoped she could keep up and that her fingers would still move with the fluidity and grace of the past. She'd tried to test herself, to practice, but really you couldn't dry-run these things. The adrenaline and myriad variables weren't things you could artificially manufacture.

She'd managed to hack into the pharmacy's system a few times and watched the workflow process through with other flu jab recipients. She'd timed the processes: figuring out the minimum and maximum tolerances and knowing just what to change and when. When all was said and done, this had turned out to be a pretty low-risk option. She didn't need to leave the comfort of her own home to attempt this and even if it failed, no one would be any the wiser.

Tracey was an impatient and ill-mannered woman. Nicole had personally witnessed her interactions in other shops—that she was not one for small-talk, or to be kept waiting. Nicole had seen the QR code on the pharmacy door; S*can here to register for your free flu immunisation today.* She was able to observe the workflows behind that QR code in real-time and with some CCTV system hacking alongside, was able to watch someone scan the code on their smartphone and begin to fill it in. The fifth question was the one: Do you have a severe allergy to egg (needing hospital care)? Nicole could follow the scripts and isolate the moment the patient clicked to submit the form and could trap it in a virtual web of her own design. The delay to the user was negligible and the pharmacist would be none the wiser. The form could be amended and sent on its way again in seconds—so long as she was there to catch it.

Tracey's electronic diary made tracking her movements easy enough. Nicole was prepared and waited behind her kitchen

18

table with increasing tension. She spotted Tracey waddling into view from the fixed camera that kept watch over the shop's door. Tracey held up her phone and scanned the door. Nicole's breathing was almost silent. She watched the workflow process entry log itself on the system—*code 3775: new item*.

Here goes...

As her mark filled in the form, Nicole waited. Not moving a muscle. Barely breathing. Eyes locked onto the video feed. The pent up, nervous energy made her fingertips tingle. It didn't take long.

Tracey looked up from her handset and moved to enter the shop. Nicole's fingers sprang into action. Her web had caught the form as planned and she scrolled through the responses, changing question five from a *Yes*, to a *No*. She pushed the form through to completion and switched cameras to the internal feed. Then she returned to her motionless, watchful position and waited.

Inside the pharmacy, Tracey stood second in line. There was a young girl at the counter and the older, male pharmacist could be just seen through the shelves to her right as she queued, but he paid her no mind. The old boy at the front of the queue was having trouble grasping the directions of his new regime of medication; the young girl evidently had little experience and was struggling to help him understand. Tracey was getting pissed off, her ample weight shifting from one hip to the other. She despised old people; they stank and were so fucking stupid all the time. And that idiot girl was useless. She huffed her impatience but it fell on deaf ears.

Moments before Tracey's entrance, the pharmacist had completed a fresh download from the local surgeries and voiced his alarm at there being another 173 prescriptions to fill.

The old boy still wasn't getting it and the girl was oblivious to Tracey. She was about to turn heel and leave when a third employee emerged from the back, all smiles and happy greetings. She took old Mr Petersen to one side to help explain it to him better. She obviously had prior dealings with Mr Petersen, as she'd recognised him instantly and made some quip about him being sweet on her as he's always in there.

This left the young girl free to serve Tracey and she tried her best to greet her with a smile.

Tracey's thunderous face made the girl visibly sag. Tracey opened her mouth to complain about the wait and the lack of apology when the pharmacist emerged from around the shelves to greet her himself. He had a tablet in his hand and it had her pre-filled form on it ready to go.

He whizzed through the questions, checking her name and date of birth but skim-read the rest; these forms were always the same and the tick boxes on this electronic form were so bloody tiny, how was he expected to read this without a magnifying glass? He was about to put the tablet down and turn to collect the vaccine when something from deep within his hippocampus pinged. He remembered this tyrant of a woman from last month. She'd given him an earful when he'd kept her waiting too long for a prescription that had only just been repeat-requested and he'd had about 50-odd others he should have been getting ready first. He hated her attitude then and it didn't look much improved now. The corner of the tablet was resting on the counter, tantalisingly close, but he brought it back up to his face again and tracked back a page.

"Miss Wolston, I need to check: have you had a flu vaccine in the past three months?" He asked her the question in full, taking his time over each word, as if he'd never spoken them aloud before.

"Of course I haven't," she snapped back, with venom.

"Did you receive the flu vaccine last winter?"

"Oh as if you don't have the records there in front of you! I have it *every* year."

Miss Wolston was looking more and more irritated with each question. Mr Petersen had left the shop and now the other two were watching her getting increasingly ticked off. They were enjoying this too. Two more questions reeled off and checked.

"What's the point filling this thing in online if you're just going to ask me everything again?" she spat.

"Miss Wolston, I must make sure the answers are all correct. Do you have a severe egg allergy—the sort that would require hospital care?"

"Yes. As. Already. Noted."

"Oh well, actually," his tone softened a bit, perhaps to be more apologetic, "It says here that you don't. Not to worry, I'll change the response for you. Janet, please could you bring me the correct vaccine for Miss Wolston?"

* * *

Nicole watched the screen as the form was pulled back into editing mode—*but not by her*—and the response changed back to *Yes*.

Dammit. Fuck's sake. Suppose that would have been too easy.
Back to the drawing board.

19

A couple of weeks went by. Things were gearing up for Christmas and there seemed to be a new email or text from the school every other day. It was really hard to keep up with them all—honestly, you'd think there was a better way to communicate with parents. Keeping up with the notable dates was exhausting and she'd already missed the day Alfie needed to bring in a cereal box and also missed the day-change for the family learning morning where she could have spent a couple of hours making outdoor tree decorations with him, as it had been moved to her day off.

On the plus side, work had levelled out again. There had not been any more unwelcome finds among the shelves—no books out of place, no makeshift bookmarks, no loiterers. The usual suspects had come and gone as they usually did.

The workshops and group meetings were exclusively Christmas-related now and paper snowflakes cut from old book pages adorned the windows. Outside in the market place, there were thousands of twinkly red, green and gold lights strung all around and, in the centre, the large Scandinavian pine. There had been a lot of hoo-ha on social media about the placement of the tree this year. Only Twynesham had reported the story last week: locals were outraged that the new position

19

meant four fewer parking spaces were available to use.

These trivial stories were driving Nicole to distraction, each one causing her far more irritation than they ever would have normally.

Normally? What does normally even mean these days?

Was it *normal* to creep around in bushes spying on people? Was it *normal* to delve into people's private lives to find vulnerabilities to exploit?

It clearly shouldn't be bloody normal. But this seemed to be Nicole's reality now.

Last week she had decided to return to the care home. There were too many unanswered questions and she figured that the care home was the most sensible place to find the answers. Tracey's home was too quiet and surrounded by other properties, whereas the care home was secluded and people were coming and going all the time. It had taken a lot of meticulous planning, and Alfie needed to be cared for late into the evening. Hayley had been more than obliging when the promise of extra cash was mooted. Nicole had left that dinnertime under the pretence of going on a date. She'd had to get all dressed up to make the ruse look convincing. She'd felt like a right berk.

She sat at the library desk, thinking back on the events from the night before.

* * *

It had been a lot of years since she'd had to drive with no headlights on—a skill she'd excelled at in training—best in class. She switched them off as she rounded the bend heading towards Dunwell. She drove along the quiet country road slowly, picking her way between the verges and trees with caution. The last thing she needed was someone to come flying along with full beams on. Driving from this direction she had to pass the main gate of the care home. She slipped by and glanced through the gateposts. Two cars were parked out front and in the dim outdoor lighting she could see they were in the designated staff spaces—and neither of them Tracey's flashy new, bright blue BMW.

She turned off the road into the loke and slowly crept along, stopping in the same place as before, beside the fallen oak.

She switched off the interior light before opening the door and climbed out into the freezing darkness. She wasn't exactly wearing the right shoes for this. She closed the car door, stopping before the door mechanism connected. She moved around to the rear door on the passenger side and slowly lifted the handle, feeling the mechanism disengage beneath her fingers. The air was so still and quiet tonight. She would have welcomed a decent wind but was thankful for the lack of rain.

She swapped her black, heeled boots for some far more sensible hiking boots, and pulled on a thick winter coat, gloves and a woolly hat—her hair be damned. As if Hayley would notice her dishevelled hair anyway. She grabbed a black holdall from the footwell and gently let that door rest almost-closed too. Leaving the car unlocked and both doors semi-open, she hoisted herself up onto the tree and over the wall for what she hoped was the very last time.

This time she had a far more audacious plan. Tracey's morning room cum office had many windows. From a security report she had found in their records online (presumably for insurance purposes), she knew how the windows were secured and knew just how to open them. She also knew, from

19

previous visits, that the nursing staff were always holed up at the opposite end of the building, where the main house met the servants' wing. She would be a long way from them and shouldn't be overheard.

Past visits had also given her the opportunity to scope out the field of vision for the motion sensors on the security lights. She'd found a dead spot. She knew that if she skirted further around the tree line from her usual place and approached the building from the east, then she would be well shielded from the security lights covering the back, as well as the light covering Tracey's private parking space to the front of the building. It was almost impossible to walk around the annexe front to back without walking through thick undergrowth and trees. The neglected gardens had grown unencumbered here, left to their own devices, providing the ideal ingress point.

Nicole had, over the preceding few weeks, begun to curate a field ops kit—never buying too many such items in one go, never from the same shop, and using cash wherever possible. She spread out the purchases and bought what she could in amongst groceries and other random household items. She bought her screwdriver set at the same time as a set of shelves and raw plugs, rather than with the crowbar or the Swiss army knife. There weren't too many things in her bag, but as with every mother, better safe than sorry.

She tentatively approached the window, pausing to make sure she was alone and that neither light would suddenly come on. Her heart pounded within her ribcage. Her whole body was trembling, but whether it was the blood pressure or the cold air, she couldn't determine. She told herself it was the cold.

Crouching down, Nicole opened her bag and placed a small head torch on over her hat. She clicked the button three times to operate in just the dim red glow of the night vision setting. She looked into the bag, contents now visible, and pulled out a stiff piece of dull grey wire. It was about half a metre long and although relatively straight, it had signs of having been repeatedly bent, dented and re-straightened. Nicole had fashioned one end of the wire into a hooked loop, and slid the wire up between the two window sashes. She had been lucky really—only one of the two brass window fasteners was fully closed. The semi-secure one she had pulled open within seconds, the other was harder. This window, since the foliage outside had gotten out of control, was clearly no longer used and the fasteners had become immobile from lack of use. She'd needed a couple of tries to get it to budge at all, but little by little, the arm started to move outwards, freeing the bottom sash from the top.

She placed her wire back in her bag, sure to leave nothing behind, and tentatively placed both gloved palms on the window pane. She applied just enough pressure to feel the pane give and began to slide the old window upwards. It was not a smooth transition; the age and old paint made the window tough to shift and the panes banged with far too high a decibel level for her comfort. She did it though.

She leant in through the open window, fists resting on the inner sill, and listened. The red light from her head torch illuminated the shapes of the furniture around her. All was peaceful.

She ducked back out and collected her bag, resting it just inside the room, and climbed in after it. Teetering on the sill, she pulled two shower caps from her pocket and covered her boots. The carpet was pale and plush, the colour distorted by the red glow. She stood up, and swivelled her head from left to right, taking in her surroundings. It was strange seeing the room from this angle. Viewing it from her old recce point, the room had taken on a two-dimensional quality—like set pieces on a stage—but now she had entered stage right.

She collected her bag from the floor and took a deep breath. Her makeshift booties made a muffled scrunching sound emanate from her feet as she made her way across to the desk. She took a moment to consider the items on the desk—nothing of much interest—and moved on to the drawers.

She opened the top drawer. Nothing interesting here, just stationery and a couple of old lipsticks. The second drawer was more interesting. Here Nicole found two yellow EpiPens in their carry case. *In case of that egg allergy presumably.* She opened them both, flicked off the blue caps and injected the epinephrine into the soft plush carpet beside her feet. She replaced the blue caps as best she could and placed them back into the carry case, and back into the drawer. *You never know—I might get lucky.*

She moved on to the bottom drawer but it was locked. She checked the top two drawers again, more meticulously this time, as well as the pots on the top of the desk. The key wasn't there. She opened her bag and took out a small black pouch. Crouching beside the drawer lock, she got to work with her tension wrench and pick. She made light work of it and replaced her tools before opening the drawer fully and inspecting the contents.

The drawer was a deep one, with the back half taken up by suspension files and the front half housing that same grey petty cash tin Nicole had seen from outside and a simple, black, soft-padded box. The petty cash tin was on top and the key was in the lock; she opened that first. Inside, she found it filled with small cardboard boxes, blister packs and bottles of various medications—all of which were prescribed and none of which sported Tracey's name. The names must have been residents there. Nicole spotted Doris, George and Alfred at first glance. She paid more attention to what the drug was. Some she recognised as pain medication, but some were completely alien to her. She took out a small pad and pencil from her other pocket and noted them down. She wrote down the patients' names too.

Nicole moved on to the black box below. There was a brass clasp on the front—a jewellery box perhaps? She lifted the lid; inside were various smaller boxes and some loose jewellery items tangled at the bottom. She straightened and rested the box on the desktop. Using both hands she looked closer at the items. The jewellery pieces appeared to be old, fine jewellery, mostly gold—rings of sapphires and rubies. It was a treasure trove of beautiful items and filled Nicole with overwhelming sadness.

As she went to replace a box housing a stunning pearl bracelet, she noticed paper underneath and could see receipts—dozens of receipts. Cautiously, she lifted them from the bottom of the box to read them better. They were from multiple jewellers, mostly in Blyworth but some in Falke and other closer towns too. Some were old, faded away to almost nothing. The one on top—clearest of all— - was a receipt from an auction house in Falke. Lot #225 from earlier in the year. Tracey'd had to pay a commission of nearly £18,000. Nicole made a mental note to look that one up later.

She replaced the contents just as she'd found them and considered the hanging files. They were all unlabelled. As Nicole made her way through them she found herself at odds with the information that was presented to her. On one hand, she felt more at ease, now that the full extent of Tracey's actions was apparent. On the other, she felt utter heartache for the victims—most of whom clearly had no idea they were being bled dry for all they were worth.

The documents here seemed to catalogue any large and lucrative asset belonging to people not named Tracey Elaine Wolston. There were papers detailing their family connections, their current state of mind, Power of Attorney documentation (all counter-signed by Gerald J. Jarvis) and covering anything from vast swathes of land overseas, to property and artwork. Seemingly, anything this woman could claim as her own was grasped with the victims completely unaware of the theft.

This must be how she's making her money—how she can buy such a property as a cash purchase.

Nicole spent much of the next hour flicking through the rest of the files. The thefts this woman was getting away with were alarming—seizing power over their estates, selling their assets from under them, stealing their medications, lying about the medications they arrived with, and faking refused doses and keeping the pills for herself. Nicole's eyes were beginning to feel the strain from the red glow of her torch and she stifled a yawn.

She turned a page and noticed a name she recognised—Iris. Iris Rawlison. Nicole's stomach contorted and she glanced up and around the room as if the wingbacked chair would offer some consolation. She read on. Iris had come into the nursing floor only two months ago after a bad fall. She'd had a stroke during the operation on her leg and now couldn't remember her own name. Iris had no living relatives and seemingly no will. Gerald had fixed that. And then Tracey had been named as Trustee of her finances and estate.

A sudden thud startled Nicole so violently that she dropped the file she was holding. Her heart pounding, she crouched and froze. The sound had been like a heavy door slamming somewhere not far from her. She closed her eyes, straining to hear a sound—anything to indicate whether she needed to flee or not.

Nicole stayed put, silent and watchful, and ruminated on what she'd found.

Iris—no! What a despicable woman Tracey was.

Nicole began her exit, careful to replace and reverse everything to be just as she'd found it, and backed her way out of the room. Even outside, after she stepped away from the window, she disturbed the ground to disguise her footprints, then made her way back to her car.

Hayley had not been at all bothered by the morose return of Nicole—not asking about her date or why she was back so early. She just took her cash and left.

Nicole flopped onto the sofa with a huff. This was the first time that she felt personally affronted by something that Tracey had done.

Personally knowing—however fleeting—one of the victims, was enough for Nicole. Tracey had sealed her fate.

20

Warfarin. Overdose of Warfarin. It'd make her blood so thin that she'd eventually start to bleed internally. Nicole had spent night after night combing through Tracey's medical records and the notes she'd made on the specific meds that Tracey had been stealing from her residents. Nicole had originally thought of exploiting the pain meds that Tracey was stealing—to up those somehow and cause her to overdose. Or she could exploit the fact that her GP would not know about the powerful Methotrexate and Naproxen she was experimenting with for her joint pain, or the Cocodomol she was taking on the side.

All these options had potential but they lacked controllable variables. Nicole could perhaps influence doses and the like but the chances of them working and giving Tracey such problems as to facilitate near-immediate death was too hard to judge.

However, the Warfarin was different. This was a medicine she took on record. It could therefore be controlled by Nicole and her keyboard.

Tracey's mechanical heart valve meant lifelong treatment and tests to keep her blood at just the right viscosity to ensure no clots formed in her heart. This also meant that Tracey's blood was already thinner than average. The trick was how to get her to up the dosage without realising.

Nicole had read dozens of practically identical correspondence from Tracey's doctors and the hospital. Every three months she was scheduled for an INR test to measure her blood viscosity. Her dosage of Warfarin was then adjusted accordingly. Her last test result was dated in October, so she would be due the next sometime in January. Tracey had stolen some stronger Warfarin tablets from Iris—little pink 5mg ones—which made the whole thing feel particularly poetic.

Nicole had worked through the scenario scrupulously, identifying the letters she would re-write and replace. The hospital would report Tracey's rising INR levels and ask the GP to lower the next dose. But the GP would receive correspondence informing him that Tracey's INR was in fact getting too low and recommending he increase her intake. Tracey, not wanting to pay for prescriptions, would hopefully continue to self-medicate using the stolen Warfarin. And so it would go on, and on, until finally, Tracey would experience the horrendous effects of serious internal haemorrhaging. Nicole would be there, ready to intercept any call made to the emergency services—preventing help from arriving. It would be too late. Within minutes, all fake letters would be replaced and traces of attempted calls would vanish into the ether. The end result *should* look as if Tracey's INR results were showing she needed a lower dose and her self-medicating antics were the cause of a gradual, fatal, build-up of Warfarin.

January seemed so far away.

* * *

20

Christmas was spent in pyjamas. They weren't ill or anything, just embracing the fact that they *could* spend all day in cosy, fleece pyjamas, cuddling, watching Home Alone and eating too many pigs-in-blankets.

Nicole felt so at ease in their pint-sized house, especially since beefing up the security measures, and loved this precious time spent with Alfie. As they sat together on the over-stuffed sofa she breathed him in, savouring every second and desperately wishing she had the ability to pause time. Time was such as cruel mistress.

A solitary tear ran down her cheek and fell into his hair. She thought about her life and struggled to remember a childhood Christmas at all—just fragments of a present here or a cracker-pull there. The people in her memories were faceless mannequins—she couldn't recall the faces of her parents any more and could barely recall the face of her brother. It explained her melancholia, yet also her determination. Determination to make sure that Alfie never experienced that same emptiness. She would always be there for him and he would never forget her face.

* * *

January.

She was awoken by an alert on her laptop. She had begun taking the thing to bed, knowing that she needed to be ready to intervene as soon as there was activity. Tracey had had her INR testing conducted the previous week in Blyworth University Hospital and the morning run of test results pinging their way across the county had begun. Nicole had found out that these were electronically sent out in batch transmissions in the early hours of the morning, and had elected to take her laptop to bed to make sure she didn't miss her opportunity.

The ping alerted her to any alterations or additions to Tracey Wolston's medical record. New test results were in. She opened the electronic letter and skim-read to the second paragraph where the letter confirmed that Tracey's INR level was a comfortable and stable 3.5, resulting in the same Warfarin prescription and dose she'd had last time and the time before that. Nicole opened the letter in a specialist program that allowed her to change the content without changing the modified information or time stamp. She replaced 3.5 with 2.0. And increased the dosage from 3mg daily to 4mg Monday to Friday and 5mg daily at weekends. She amended the ending of the letter by asking Tracey to contact the hospital for a follow-up test in a month's time.

Simple.

A couple of days later, Nicole checked the pharmacy records to see whether the higher dose had been prescribed before waiting once more—biding her time. All the earlier foreboding and agitation were mysteriously lifted of late—the fog gone, her mind clear and calculating. She wasn't worrying about the blackmailer or the crimes she was about to commit. She couldn't recognise it herself, but she was losing her grip on her sanity.

It had begun.

21

Two weeks had passed and Nicole was ready for Act Two. All the while, she had been keeping watch on the records, checking Tracey attended the blood test appointment accordingly, waiting for the next letter to ping in.

At 3 am on a Thursday, Nicole was woken by the alert and propped herself up in bed to make similar adjustments to the new letter. This time the hospital lab reported that Tracey's INR level was 6.3 and she needed urgent remedial action from the GP to significantly reduce her regular dose of Warfarin.

Nicole switched the narrative; changing 6.3 to 2.5 and making the GP think she needed urgent remedial action with a greatly *elevated* dose of an anti-coagulant. She removed the automated workflow generating a follow-up appointment.

Another fortnight passed. Tracey's INR was moving up and up, beyond 7 now for sure. Her GP, under the impression it was a tad too low, was continuing to further increase her Warfarin dose. *It won't be long now.*

* * *

Tracey began this Tuesday with a spring in her step. She was leaving the offices of Gerald J. Jarvis and couldn't stop grinning. Actually, it would be better described as a smirk. *It had bloody well worked.*

She was now the proud owner of the most gorgeous country farmhouse and she hadn't had to spend a penny of her own money. It was fucking hilarious—how easy this all was. *Those doddery old twats who get brought in and haven't a clue where their own fucking pisshole is...like taking sweets off a baby. Well, it is when you have another old fart doing the legal stuff.* Despite the cut Gerald took, she'd been making a killing.

Tracey crossed over to the surface car park in the centre of Falke and squeezed her paunchy belly between her beemer and an Audi, the keychain on her bag scraping mercilessly against the door panels of the Audi's dark grey immaculate finish. She also didn't hold back when squeezing her ample rear into the driver's seat, repeatedly thumping door against the door panel.

As she landed heavily in the low-slung driver's seat and plonked her mammoth handbag on the passenger's, she howled in agony. Her pounding head and nausea from her hangover was bad enough, but she'd been having these weird pains in her lower gut all morning. She grimaced as she experienced another now. Her face contorted and she struggled to breathe. She gripped the steering wheel hard whilst she waited for the feeling to pass. With her eyes clamped shut against the wall of pain, she reached over to her bag and plunged her hand in to find something. Rummaging around she located what she was after and pulled out a half-used blister pack of Naproxen. She popped two and washed them down with her Starbucks cappuccino. The pain subsided to a dull ache. She breathed heavily now, angry that this pain was interfering with her otherwise fantastic morning.

21

Ramming the car into gear, she skidded out of the car park and made her way south towards Dunwell. Honestly, she couldn't stop grinning. She was in high spirits once more.

As she pulled into the main gate, she glanced left towards the parking area. In the staff spaces were a moped with L plates, and a small Fiat with rusty edges and a Shrek head topping the antenna. She smirked. *These fucking plebs I have to manage... I can't wait to ditch this place.* She swerved her beemer violently to the right and followed an unmarked narrow track which took her behind the tree line and towards her office annexe—and a small one-car parking space all of her own.

She parked up and climbed out—another wave of gut pain causing her legs to buckle. She only stopped herself from falling by grabbing the car door. A moment passed and the pain subsided again. *Fucking meds.*

She waddled in through a floor-length window-cum-door so that she wouldn't have to chance bumping into anyone by using either of the other entrances. She hated the rest of the building and would only venture out there when it was completely unavoidable.

The rest of the morning was spent daydreaming about interiors from the comfort of her office. She scrolled through endless Pinterests, occasionally pausing to save one. During a brief break in her scrolling, she looked up and glanced around the room, admiring her hand-picked décor choices. She really liked it in here. The plush interior made her feel important; she felt regal. She was the queen and the staff and residents were merely her subjects and servants—there to do her bidding. She craved the power, the authority. She thrived on it. She was going to miss it. She considered for the briefest of moments whether she really should give up this gig—it was so lucrative.

One of the younger carers rapped on the door and started to open it.

"Sorry Miss Wolston, but there's a visitor at the front desk and—"

"Did I tell you to come in?" she barked, outraged by the audacity and the interruption.

"No...erm...sorry, I..." the girl was scared and floundering. Tracey liked it.

"Why the fuck do I care if there's someone here?" she interrupted.

The girl looked at the floor, but bravely continued. "Well, he wants to visit his Gran. She's upstairs in Room 14, but she hasn't been washed for a couple of days."

Tracey just stared at her, her face maintaining a look of utter contempt. *Fuck's sake I don't need this shit any more.*

"Well tell him to get lost. Tell him she's having a bath right now and that he'd better make an appointment next time or something. For Christ's sake girl think for yourself. Leave me in peace."

Tracey waved her hand dismissively at the quavering girl who hurriedly retreated and closed the door behind her. Tracey winced at a sharp pain in her stomach—she was going to be sick. She moved with more speed than she'd exhibited in years, lucky that there was a small toilet adjacent to her office—an add-on she'd insisted upon. *She wasn't going to share a toilet with these disgusting piss-soaked old trouts.*

Tracey flew in and just got to the toilet bowl in time as thick, dark vomit expelled from her mouth, covering the seat, lid back and cistern. It hit the wall and porthole window beyond too. It stank and looked like black coffee-grounds. She was so confused. She could taste the metallic liquid and felt it coating

21

her teeth and tongue. It made her gag. Her stomach convulsed again and she couldn't hold it in. She was bent double on the floor, head in the bowl, bloody thick paste oozing out and drooling down her chin in long, sticky trickles. She tried to wipe it away with the back of her hand but it only smeared across her cheek. She was breathing hard and the pain inside her was spreading—it was coming from everywhere now. She started to cry—sobs gurgling with the gritty, coffee-like substance in her throat.

Low down in her abdomen, the pain intensified. She frantically pulled herself up and tried to get back out into the office. She was panicking and all she could think about was getting to her phone. She vomited again. *My beautiful, silken velvet £89 per square metre...* On all fours now, she clutched at a dry area of carpet, staining it. Unable to control anything, she just let the foul substance dribble out of her mouth as she heaved in shaky, spluttering breaths.

She reached out for the handle of her bag and yanked on it just as another wave of excruciating pain flooded over her. Her bag tipped, spilling the contents into the puddle between her arms.

She failed repeatedly to unlock her phone, the bloody coffee-grounds rendering her fingerprint useless. She curled up into a ball on that lavish, sage-green carpet and finally dialled 999. Her hands were shaking terribly as she brought the phone to her ear and began to silently weep, unable to do much else.

The cool, calm voice of the operator rang loud in her ear. "You're through to Emergency Services, which service do you require?"

Between faltering breaths, Tracey answered, "Ambulance."

"Please hold on a moment, I'm putting you through now."

The wait was interminable. Tracey's stomach was in a near-permanent state of spasm now. Eventually, a bright, friendly voice crackled onto the line. "You're through to the ambulance service, what is your emergency?"

"I'm sick... I'm... urgh... I'm vomiting blood. The pain..." Tracey could barely utter this at little more than a whisper—the pain sapping her lungs of air.

"Can you tell me your name?" replied the soothing voice.

"Tracey. Wolston." Her surname barely a whisper.

"Okay Tracey, I need to you tell me where you are so I can dispatch an ambulance to your location. Can you manage that?"

Between heavy breaths and rattling sobs, Tracey conveyed the address of Clandon House. The operator promised to stay with her until the ambulance arrived.

"Don't you worry, Tracey, the ambulance will be there soon."

Tracey could only respond with another bout of vomiting. The pain was immense and her thoughts weren't coherent any longer. She could only make strange noises and her hands were too weak to hold the phone up. It slid from her hand and sat in the bloody vomit which was pooling around her now-reposed head. She could hear the faint voice of the operator calling out her name, over and over, asking her if she could still hear her. Tracey's vision blurred and her eyes stung as her abdomen convulsed again and her body shuddered. In that last moment of lucidity, Tracey was sure she heard the name Iris. Her phone screen went dark and then came to rest on the call screen, 999 punched in but the call not sent—but she didn't notice.

Tracey wasn't going to notice anything any more.

22

That lunchtime, Nicole cleaned house. The documents on Tracey's medical records were changed back to their original state and documented an INR level that was spiralling upwards and that Tracey's doses of Warfarin were getting lower to compensate. Tracey's phone records were also adjusted—it would look like Tracey reached her phone, keyed in 999 but was unable to manage dialling out.

It was regrettable that someone was going to have to find her in that state, but what can you do?

* * *

Over the next few days, the story was picked up in the local press, with subsequent follow-ups revealing the intricacies of her fraud, theft and general nasty ways. Her solicitor was now being sought out to answer questions, but he'd vanished. The coroner ruled her death *accidental, caused by gastrointestinal haemorrhage*—noting Tracey's self-medication of Warfarin which was in higher dosages than her prescribed pills. She was the talk of the town for many weeks thereafter, although Nicole wasn't following the story any more. Not that she wasn't interested—she was very interested, indeed most interested to keep abreast of any suspicions, but her attention was diverted.

Diverted by the series of books she'd found in the library. Books with notes. Books with bookmarks.

This wasn't over.

23

A week had gone by since Nicole had found the next set of books left for her in the library. At first, she just ignored them and left them on the shelves, untouched for the remainder of that day. She told herself she had other jobs to get on with and ignored them until after lunch. She couldn't shake their presence from her mind and began to fret that a customer would pick one up or move them. The possible consequences of ignoring the message then started to settle in, like a sea fog rolling towards her, standing motionless on the shore.

She felt restless and distracted, unable to focus on her work. Her muscles were twitchy and her mind was in turmoil. It was just as an afternoon macramé class began that Nicole finally relented.

Within a minute, she had collected up the three books she'd spotted earlier and checked them out, depositing them in her tote beside her feet under the desk. She felt relieved in an unsettling sort of way and was able to carry out her duties, but she was also upset—more upset and distressed than she'd been in a good many years. It unnerved her, this unapologetic return of a feeling that she hadn't experienced for so long. How quickly it had returned. She wondered if she'd ever feel normal again.

* * *

That night, Nicole lay awake. She hadn't given any consideration to the books in her tote downstairs. She was consumed by the mix of emotions gurgling around her, and struggled to clear the fog and remember the meditation techniques her therapist had helped her develop. None of it was working.

BANG!

The sudden and earth-shattering sound was like an electric shock to her chest. She sat bolt upright in bed, blood pulsing through her ears making it impossible to hear. *What was that?* She strained to hear, listening for more sounds—any sounds other than her own physiological reactions. *Is that a baby crying?* She heard a wooden stair creak. *Second stair on the left side.* Someone was coming up the stairs. She froze. She couldn't move, she was just staring at the gap in the doorway, waiting. Another stair creaked—this one much quieter. But she recognised it—five stairs from the top. She could barely breathe, each expelled breath making her lungs shrink until she couldn't fill them again. Tears were rolling down her face unchecked. But still she couldn't move.

Alfie.

She was suddenly aware of a dark, shadowed figure at the doorway—the door slowly swinging back on its hinges to reveal the dark shape in all its horror. With startling speed, the shadow crossed to the bed and climbed on top of her, throwing her back and half burying her head between the pillows. She screamed, but she heard nothing.

Alfie!

Her heart ached. As her eyes stuck wide open, she could only stare, mouth agog. The dark shadow expanded into a mass of black, swirling smoke covering her and the bed. She was terrified. The pressure on her chest was so heavy now, she couldn't breathe in at all. Her vision faded to black.

BANG!

A sudden, loud sound startled her awake and she sat bolt upright in bed. She drew in deep, long, lungfuls of air.

It was just a dream.

She felt like crying. But the noise... *there had been a noise, right?* She was trembling all over from the nightmare—her heart beating so violently she thought she'd pass out. *Was there a noise?*

She climbed out of bed on unsure legs and crossed to the bedroom door. Pulling it open, she looked out into the hallway. Nothing. There was nothing. She padded along the floorboards, stepping cautiously from rug to rug, and listened in at Alfie's door. She could hear his snuffly breaths. *All okay.*

Unexpectedly her legs buckled and she sank down onto the cold floor. Hugging her knees, she bowed her head and silently sobbed.

24

It was late February now. The nights were long and dark. This used to be Nicole's favourite time of year. She liked the quiet of February. December was chaotic and busy and crammed. January was gloomy and full of people clinging on to something: New Years resolutions and *seize the day* mentality that drove her bonkers. February was different. February was quiet. By February, people had stopped banging on about their resolutions—they'd either given up by now or were bored talking about them. February was cold and often brought snow. Nicole loved the snow. *Maybe I should have relocated to Scotland.* The muted, softness of the sounds around after a heavy snowfall brought such comfort to Nicole. It wasn't unlike a sound-proofed chamber to her.

She stood at the glazed back door, looking out into the garden. It was dusk and the light had that sepia quality, indicating snow. She nursed a cup of tea and pondered the weather.

Alfie was playing in his room upstairs—she could hear him now, shooting Hot Wheels cars across the room. A minuscule movement caught her eye. She noticed a speck, then another. The snowflakes fell with unexpected heaviness, blanketing the small lawn within minutes. She opened the door, inviting in the cold and the smell. She held out her hand and let some fall into her palm. The atmosphere out here was already so peaceful and calm.

Bliss.

In the weeks immediately following Tracey Wolston's demise, Nicole had struggled to get a handle on things. Her PTSD, that she had worked so very hard to manage, had floored her. Images from six years ago were playing each night in her head like some sick movie reel—the fear she had experienced, the trauma and interrogation. Night after night she woke, drenched in sweat and screaming—the deafening wail of baby's cries still reverberating around her. Every night she would end up at Alfie's door, sobbing into her knees. She replayed the horrific events she had lived through and felt how precariously close she was to being taken back there.

From conception to when she first held him in her arms, she had been a wreck. A wreck that almost ended his treasured life before it had begun. She had been rendered utterly impotent with paranoia after her ordeal. She couldn't function. The agency she worked for decommissioned her almost immediately, labelling her indefinitely unfit to be out in the field or even in a mission room. *Untrustworthy* and *Unstable* were cited. She had been devastated and it served as a catalyst for her already plummeting mental state and ability to trust. She'd even convinced herself at one point that her therapist wasn't to be trusted either.

It had been a very lonely place. A frightening place. And now it seemed as though all the good work she'd put in to move past these horrific trials had been for nothing.

No. It wasn't for nothing. She had to keep telling herself that.

There were many good reasons—all of them involving Alfie.

He was her rock—the only thing that stopped her from losing her grip on everything. He kept her grounded and she must therefore keep him safe at all costs.

If she could just get a handle on these nightmares. They transported her straight back, as if a day hadn't passed since, and she relived every dreadful day of captivity and abuse. She couldn't forget a single part of the harrowing torture, stress positions and sleep deprivation.

There was a distant part of her that knew she was doing wrong, but the louder part of her brain was fogging up her moral compass. There was a part of her that relished the chance to do harm to another person, a person who was doing harm to others—she had to protect those who couldn't protect themselves. No one was protecting *her* all those years ago. But by doing this on their behalf—on behalf of those unable to help themselves—then it was as if she were balancing the books. It might not make sense to most, but to Nicole, this was arguably an entirely acceptable trade-off.

And this blackmailer clearly knew this. She knew just how to get under Nicole's skin. Just how to put her on edge and to instil fear in her again—how to invoke this murderous desire to right wrongs. This blackmailer knew too much and didn't care for the consequences to Nicole. She was merely a pawn.

And she hadn't got to her endgame yet.

Nicole closed her palm around the snowflakes with renewed determination. She closed the door, retrieved her tote bag and got to work.

25

The three books sat in front of her now, laid out side-by-side on the table top. A steaming mug of tea sat top right.

She picked up the first: *Far from the Madding Crowd* by Thomas Hardy. It had a bookmark placed at page 123. The copy was an old 1980s print, the cover worn and faded, sporting a painting of a flock of sheep in a snowy woodland lane. There were so many pages given up to the introduction, maps and other such front matter, that the story didn't even begin until page fifty-one. Page 123 was midway through the ninth chapter.

It had been decades since Nicole had read this, but she remembered enjoying the story and the formidable female lead of Bathsheba. Page 123 began with the trample of horses hooves signalling the arrival of Mr Boldwood into the story. Nicole tried to recall Mr Boldwood, sure that he was the lonely neighbouring farmer who was sent a Valentine by Bathsheba in jest, but who then, rather awkwardly, falls for her.

Nicole replaced the book on the table and picked up the second: *The Girl on the Train* by Paula Hawkins. Nicole had read this book only a couple of years previously and remembered it well. The cover of this edition sported the tagline: "You don't know her. But she knows you." *Eerily apodictic.*

The storyline primarily follows a woman named Rachel. Her marriage had ended—caused largely by her alcoholism and inability to conceive. She frequently binges and blacks out. And discovers the horrific things she has done whilst drunk that she has no memory of.

The third novel was an Agatha Christie whodunnit: *A Murder is Announced*. Nicole had read many Christies over the years but leaned towards Poirot, rather than Marple. She hadn't read this one. She read the blurb and inspected the exterior. Nothing of particular note here—the peach, stylised front cover and Agatha's scrawled signature not really giving anything away other than a gun being involved.

Nicole lifted out the scrap of paper tucked inside the front cover. It was blank except for five letters, arranged downwards on the paper. At the top sat the letter "T" on its own. Next line down were the letters "T T", and below those the letters "D M".

Hmm...

Nicole pondered these letters and spent some time considering their possible meanings and the evidently deliberate arrangement upon the paper. Nothing sensible presented itself to her. She considered the possibility of having to take the time to read this one—time she might not have. She took a slurp of tea, closed her eyes and tried to clear her head.

The air in the room around her began to thicken. All the negative, empty space became more solid than the wooden table in front of her. This heavy, thick, invisible weight was bearing down on her. She felt microscopic. Her muscles tightened. *I need to move.* She shot up from the table and paced the room, shaking her head, trying to dislodge the sensation. Repeatedly she screwed up her eyes and released them, expecting the darkness pressing in from left and right to dissipate. It wouldn't relent.

She knew in that moment that she was losing the battle. Her eyes were scratchy and bothering her.

Ignoring the books laid out on the table she strode out of the room and into the cooler, darker hallway. She paused momentarily to look towards the front door, checking it was secure, before mounting the stairs.

She needed to rest. She needed to *sleep*.

* * *

The nightmares stayed away that night. Work was terribly busy the following day and she spent much of the morning fire-fighting against things gone wrong and people needing assistance. Nicole was barely given time to think. Which turned out to be a good thing. The distractions—lasting all day—were just what she needed. It was 8:24 pm before she realised she hadn't thought about the books, or her situation, all day. This perked her up immensely.

She felt some semblance of control again.

That small glimmer of respite was all she needed to clear her thoughts and approach matters with a fresh eye. And a fresh head.

By 8:26 pm she was once more sitting at her kitchen table, with her notebook, pen and selection of books laid out before her. But this time, things were different. The serenity she'd found in her overly busy day had put a whole new complexion on things. She was filled with a newfound resolve, but also intrigue. She wanted to find the answer. She *needed* to find the answer. She needed to solve the riddle and put the jigsaw pieces together.

She picked up *The Girl on the Train* again and, ignoring the taunting tagline, opened the book's front cover. She flipped through the first couple of pages and paused at the dedication page. There, the author's simple dedication, "For Kate", had been crossed out and amended. *In pen!* There was a momentary sting of librarian outrage, replaced instantly with curiosity when Nicole became aware of something pushing up the page from the other side. Upon investigation, she found a small stamp-sized square of paper tucked fast into the crease of the book on the following page.

The paper had one word written on it: *Rachel*.

She needed to start making notes. Sliding her notebook towards her, she began to jot things down on a fresh page:

> *Far from the Madding Crowd* – p123
> Mr Boldwood enters story.
> Liddy, Coggan, Maryann, Bathsheba Everdene
> Farmers? Estates?
>
> *The Girl on the Train*
> Rachel? MC – alcoholic? Divorced? Blackouts?
> Rachel surname – Watson
>
> *A Murder is Announced* – Christie
> Miss Marple
> T, T T, D M

25

Bloody hell, this isn't much to go on, she thought to herself. Stumped, she flicked on the kettle. She watched the water through the clear glass—still and tinted blue from the LEDs. She made a mental note to do something about the limescale. *It's so bad here.*

Nicole accepted that she needed to read this Agatha Christie one. She relocated to the sofa, tea in hand. With something of a disgruntled huff, she settled down to read. She had barely reached the end of the first page before bells were going off in her head. She jumped up, tea spots spilling on her jeans, and read the passage again:

> *Between 7:30 and 8:30 every morning except Sundays, Johnnie Butt made the round of the village... yadda yadda... alighting at each house or cottage to shove through the letterbox such morning papers as had been ordered... yadda yadda... at Miss Blacklock's he left the **T**elegraph, **T**he **T**imes and the **D**aily **M**ail.*

T, T T, D M. Nicole checked the papers received by the other village inhabitants visited by Johnnie Butt each morning except Sundays. No one else received this combination of papers. She couldn't believe it. This was marvellous—she didn't have to read the whole thing after all. Hell, she didn't even need to read the first chapter.

Nicole moved back to the kitchen and resettled at the table, adding *Letitia Blacklock* to her notes. Still not a great deal to go on, but maybe, just maybe, this was all she needed.

26

Nicole slept tremendously that night. She was elated. She had solved the riddles and clues, and now had a name.

Well, admittedly she had a few names. Her programme written for Miss Wolston received an update last night and the resulting list of names vanished, to be replaced by a new set. These were names connected with all the keywords Nicole had noted down earlier that evening.

The most likely candidate, from a geographic standpoint, was a farmer who ran Blacklock Farm on the west side of Twynesham. His name was Robert Lock and he was in his early sixties.

He had a younger brother David, who was in his late fifties. There didn't appear to be anyone else connected with this pair—not surviving anyway. Their father was the tenant farmer before them and the older brother Robert succeeded the tenancy some 20 years before. Neither of them married; no kids or other relatives. Oh, but possibly a dog. At least, there was a young-looking Dutch Shepherd pictured beside them in photos from *Young Farmers* articles from a few years back. Seems Grandfather Lock was a founding member of the Norfolk contingency, and David and Robert were dragged back for ceremonial purposes from time to time. Blacklock Farm

26

had a long-standing contract with British Sugar and certainly *used to* supply a sizeable proportion of the sugar beet processed at their Wissington factory since the 1930s. Although in recent years the yield had lessened considerably. The hardship of farming a 114 hectare farm on their own evidently took its toll on the Lock brothers.

The only elements that didn't fit were the Rachel clues—neither Lock was divorced and there were no discernible connections to a Watson. Which left the alcoholic element.

Nicole wanted to find out about this Robert; her instincts were telling her that this was an area that needed fleshing out. If there was perhaps some bad blood between them, or some leverage that she could exploit, then all the better.

It took little time to find answers. The first article Nicole came across was brief, but informative. It was dated a few years back, and detailed a conviction against Robert Lock that previous month, explaining that he received a suspended sentence for causing death by careless driving—suspended largely in part because of his unblemished record and the negligible risk he posed to the public. The journalist did use that platform to continue for some paragraphs on the state of Norfolk prisons and overcrowding being the real root of the high proportion of suspended sentences being handed out lately.

Nicole dug further into the careless driving incident. It was local so there was *a lot* that the local press had to say. Seven years earlier, an accident on the far western edge of Blacklock Farmland, a tractor—driven by Robert—was hauling a trailer carrying sugar beet. The trailer was being reversed out of a field through a narrow gap in the hedgerow, into a narrow country road.

The earliest article she could find was from Blyworth Evening News and read:

> *This is the scene in Twynesham after an eight-year-old boy died following a collision with a tractor. The boy was hit by the vehicle on a farm this afternoon.*
>
> *Sadly, he was pronounced dead at the scene.*
>
> *A police officer is standing guard at the scene off Station Road, while forensic crime scene investigators gather evidence to explain how this tragedy might have unfolded. The boy's family are being supported by specialist officers.*
>
> *A police spokesperson said the driver of the tractor is being cooperative and assisting with their enquiries.*

Further articles went on to detail that Robert had been in control of the vehicle at the time and it was chalked up to just a terrible accident. He was charged with careless driving, the possibility of being distracted at the wheel being the prosecution's key argument. He was sentenced to five years in prison, but the sentence was suspended.

His conviction caused a farm ownership struggle. The Midrake family attempted to use that as leverage to claim a tenancy breach. The Locks nearly lost the farm that year. *That would explain the animosity between families and their spat in the pub.*

Nicole was also irritated by the low level of detail the press reports gave. She knew they knew more than they were letting on and it made her so mad. It seemed like the reporters had sat around mocking the "public" for being so ignorant of the truth. *Why couldn't they just report everything and let us make up our own minds about things?*

Nicole wanted to know everything. And the best place to get all the sublime details were the police files. Gone were the days of having to have some corruptible informant who would 'borrow' the file for you, nowadays it was remarkably easy to hack in and find what you were after—*if* you knew what it was you were looking for.

And Nicole knew, but could never have guessed what she'd find.

27

Police files always made for a fascinating read. Because the case went to trial, there were a significant quantity of documents to wade through. Almost everything related to Robert Lock and his confession. Detailed plans of the area it happened in, the specifications of the tractor and trailer, blindspots, whether the radio was on, what activity was going on on his mobile phone at the time—that sort of intricate detail. Far back in the very early stages of the investigation were some documents and pages that were far more interesting.

There were a few pages of photocopies, each one capturing sequential pages in a police officer's pocketbook. The bottom centre of each page was annotated with the PC's badge number, building a picture of the officer's day. This officer was PC598 - Lydia Coggan. A quick index search informed Nicole that Lydia had only been in the job a few months when she got this call out. She'd happened to have been the closest officer at the time, attending a call out in Twynesham about a stolen garden gnome.

Her first photocopied pages detailed her observations of the scene and the immediate aftermath, including canvassing some isolated houses on the lane for witnesses. There was an older woman living in the nearest house to the incident. She

27

had come out to gawp, claiming she saw it happen and that it wasn't Robert driving. But this notation was the only mention of this fact in the whole file. It wasn't followed up, it wasn't even elaborated on in the pocketbook. This Ethel Barrett was never questioned on it or asked to make a formal statement. Robert's confession was all that anyone had paid any attention to.

If not Robert, then ...?

A few documents along from the pocketbook copies, Nicole found the detail she craved. The boy's family was with him at the time of the incident; he and his younger sister were on scooters and the others were on foot. The Hargreaves had just gone out for a walk and had stuck to the roads to give the children the chance to use their scooters. The children were therefore naturally slightly ahead of the walking party.

Alexander Hargreaves, being older, had shot off at speed—his younger sister Lily, only six at the time, being more reticent of the sloping road ahead. The children were estimated to have been somewhere between 120-150 metres ahead of the adults when a large trailer full of beet began to emerge from the tall, thick hedgerow to the right of the road. Alexander had stopped to wait for his sister. The driver didn't see him and Alexander didn't notice he was in danger. The trailer ploughed straight into him. His sister's screams were what alerted the driver apparently. The trailer came to a sudden halt and began to move forward again, as the rest of the family got to him.

The reports suggested Alexander died instantly from massive brain injuries. His mother and father attempted to resuscitate him but it was no use. Lily was noted as standing much further along the road accompanied by the grandmother, Mrs Cynthia Bishop. It was mentioned in her witness statement that it had taken the three adults half a minute to get to the accident site from where they were, but that the younger sister had mentioned another man being close by behind the hedgerow. Again, this wasn't followed up or mentioned again.

A picture was being painted here—a picture far different to the one that resided in Robert's confessional statement. Who was this mystery man lurking nearby? And why would he need to lurk about at all? Why would you hide? *Because you are guilty. What if Robert wasn't driving the tractor... what if it was David? Why would Robert confess?... To protect his younger brother? Why protect David? Why risk your freedom?*

Nicole searched further into David Lock. The younger Lock had a record of his own and it was a lot more colourful and lengthy than Robert's. There were many citations and notes in his summary on vehicular stops and breathalyser results. Lost licence points and two years before this incident, he was banned from driving for four years. *So he wouldn't have a valid licence at the time of the incident.* This was starting to fit together now. If David was driving, without a licence, and coming out from the farmland onto a public highway, then he would have been in a lot more trouble than his brother. He would have been charged with more than just careless driving—going away for a lot longer than Robert would have with his otherwise clean record. And he'd faced a negligible chance of a suspended sentence.

And it seemed pretty likely that David Lock had probably been drinking too—there were multiple drunk-and-disorderly and drink-driving mentions for many years before the incident, increasing in regularity afterwards too. He would have likely been convicted of causing death by dangerous driving, driving without a licence, driving under the influence... probably more.

27

All this seemed entirely plausible as reason enough for sensible Robert to take the rap for this awful incident.

Nicole sat back and took a moment to think. The diminutive, fragile body of eight-year-old Alexander Hargreaves left an impression in her vision like a negative image dancing around in front of her. She thought of Alfie and felt weak.

The self-destructive, selfish and downright horrific behaviour displayed by this David Lock was making her blood boil.

She needed to see this man in the flesh.

She needed to look him in the eye.

28

A few days passed. It was now the first weekend of March. Springtime. And under the pretence of a rejuvenating walk, Nicole and Alfie made their way west.

Nicole had scoped out the accident site prior to this visit and knew just where to park so that their walk could begin shortly before the crest of the hill Alexander and Lily had scooted down that fateful day. Alfie was always full of energy so he didn't need much encouragement to head out.

The day was bright and dry, but still satisfactorily cold. Greenery was back and the grass verges were peppered with snowdrops and the beginnings of yellow daffodils. They walked over the hill crest and began the slow walk down the lane. Nicole tried to picture the scene that day: how far off those children must have been from their parents, how quickly they could have reached the hedge gap and what they might have been able to see from their vantage point. From there, further up the hill, Nicole could surmise that the tractor itself would very much be hidden from view, as the hedge created significant difficulties for anyone pulling out of there. As the pair neared the gap, Nicole could assess the thickness of the hedge, and height of it, and how it would easily obscure a person standing on the other side. It would have been impossible to know who was driving, so no wonder Robert's proclamation wouldn't likely be questioned.

Nicole and Alfie walked on. From the maps she'd looked at prior to this jaunt out, Nicole knew that there was a narrow public footpath running alongside this field to their right, which weaved its way towards the main body of Blacklock Farm—not the front of it, the Station Road facing entrance, but the back one. The back, where all the farm equipment and additional farm buildings were.

They found the footpath entrance with minimal fuss, the wooden signpost cleared of weeds by some regular user. The path was narrow but well-used. Along its course, it crossed many farm tracks, allowing movement between fields without the need for public highway use.

As they approached one of these tracks she heard the unmistakeable growl of a diesel engine—a big one. It was getting a lot louder and Alfie saw it before she did.

"Look Mummy!"

She wheeled around to watch as the imposing form of a massive green tractor, made larger by its proximity, rumbled past, hugging the field edge no more than two metres from where they stood. It made Nicole feel a sudden insecurity. She looked up towards the cab and recognised the profile of David Lock—not much different from the mug shots, just more jowly and more unkempt.

Within seconds he had passed. Alfie wanted to chase the tractor. He wasn't even as tall as the yellow wheel inners but still tried to run alongside to keep up with it. But there was no fence along the next section and Nicole was terrified that he'd come careering through the narrow hedge and flatten Alfie. She sprinted to grab him and stop him. He wasn't happy with her intervention and struggled to break free from her grasp. They continued walking, but the mood was soured. Alfie was sulking and Nicole was uneasy.

They rounded a corner and could see the rooftops of a collection of buildings across the field from where they now stood. The public footpath followed the tree line round to the right, but she wanted to head out left, right across the field, to get a better view of the farmhouse.

"Come on Alfie, we're going this way." She indicated a route straight through the field. Alfie looked at her with disdain.

"I want to go home," he said, with more than a little petulance in his tone.

"Well, we will soon, but first Mummy wants to look at something over here. Don't you want to see the tractor again?" she tried to tempt him.

Alfie didn't answer her but began to walk in the direction she wanted him too, so she chalked that up to a win. She fell in line behind him as they slowly tracked diagonally across the field, making straight for the farm buildings. She could see a green and yellow tractor parked beside a modern built barn—presumably the same one that passed them earlier.

As they neared the farm she could make out the layout better. They were approaching from the north, where the majority of the outbuildings, store rooms and barns were. There was a large, wooden gate leading out into the field and splitting left and right, presumably to head off to other parts of the land. The gate was open, and Nicole could see the track cut through the middle of the farm. It was a grassy track, with grassy verges either side so that the parts worn down by tyres were drawing a double stripe through the green. The buildings flanked this track, and as the pair got closer they adjusted their course to

28

the left to intercept the track leading directly from the farm and be square-on to the view between the buildings. From this vantage she could see the house, sitting at the far end, where the double stripe ended. She could see the nose of another tractor—a red one—poking out from a barn to the right.

"Is there suffin oi cen help you wiv?" said a pleasant, rumblingly low-tone voice from behind them.

Nicole and Alfie both jumped at the sudden intrusion and Nicole wheeled round to face the opposite direction. There in front of her, not four metres away, stood Robert Lock. He looked markedly older than the photographs she had become so familiar with.

"Oh, no, no—nothing. We were just going for a walk and got a bit turned about. I was, erm...".

Robert Lock's face looked awfully suspicious. But it softened when Alfie spoke up.

"I wanted to see the tractor." Nicole could have kissed him.

"Oh is that roight? Well tha's my bruvver's one that is. So I wu'nt be gorn over there. You dint want t'mess wi' 'im."

"We're sorry, we'll head back to try and find the footpath," said Nicole placatingly.

"Tha's roight, you be orn y'way." And with that Robert Lock stalked off towards the farm with not another glance back at them.

He shut the gate behind him.

29

As they got back to their car, Nicole pondered this warning of Robert's. She wondered whether finding out more about the relationship between the two brothers was of any consequence. Good or bad, what difference would it ultimately make to the task in front of her now?

Their walk that afternoon hadn't just been to set eyes on Lock. It had been to assess the stage they were currently at with their sugar beet farming as well. She had found out that March was the month for drilling the sugar beet and before that the ground was usually twice cultivated. The fields they had walked through hadn't yet been touched at all since the barren winter period. This meant that very soon there was likely to be a flurry of activity to get the fields ready for drilling.

With just the two of them to manage this, there was certainly going to be some seriously heavy machinery in use. Nicole had thankfully managed to get close enough to the farm to check the tractor David was using in more detail. It was perhaps the most modern piece of kit in sight, certainly more technological than she could have ever hoped for.

That evening, with Alfie in bed, she was able to do a little more digging into the intricacies of tractor programming. Before long, Nicole stumbled across a news story about Russians stealing 27 pieces of John Deere farming equipment from a dealer in Ukraine and shipping them off to Chechnya. It was lauded as a hoot that John Deere was able to reach out over the internet and remotely initiate a kill switch in-built into the brand new machines, rendering them completely inert and raising concerns on cyberwarfare and the corruptible power held by large corporations in general.

This was obviously terribly concerning to the farming industry—that if a John Deere technician can reach out and kill any machine anywhere in the world, then so too can the Russian storied hacker army. But it was music to Nicole's ears. There was no doubt whatsoever that she would be able to take control of Lock's tractor. *But what to do with it then?*

No time like the present.

It took Nicole less than three hours to hack into the John Deere servers. They had enhanced encryption that she hadn't come up against for some years, but it was nothing she couldn't handle. The integrated reciprocal contingency encryption was a cryptography code she had helped develop herself, so all in all it was a relatively quick infiltration process.

What was evident was that she could pinpoint the precise location of any John Deere tractor or combine and indeed, initiate that built-in kill switch the article had been talking about; but the other control parameters for the equipment was housed locally. Each licensed user had access to a dashboard interface called the CommandCenter. It was this piece of kit that would allow Nicole to control the tractor whilst in use. It also meant that she could build security walls behind her, so any diagnostics run from John Deere itself would show nothing untoward.

Nicole arched her back, cracking the lower vertebrae and

formed a mental to-do list. She flexed her fingers, hovering just over the soft-type keys and got to work.

30

The plan was clear in her mind now.

It had taken a few days of painstaking preparation—building a parallel security wall to hide all of her activity from the programmers. It was like taking a section of footage and looping it, the watcher unaware that something entirely different was going on in reality. Nicole had taken the pre-programmed scheduling input at the Lock farm's computer interface and plotted it against a regular calendar. It gave her a fair estimation of where that tractor was going to be on any given day and time. She could tell by the programme setup which piece of machinery was required for each part of this process too—an invaluable addition to the automated setup. The only thing it couldn't tell her was which brother was in the driving seat.

There were seven primary opportunities for this plan to work. Seven scheduled cultivation runs were planned over the coming two weeks—at least, seven that were scheduled to use the rotavator.

Last week she had bought Alfie a gift. It wasn't his birthday, or Christmas or anything, but they had been watching an episode of Dennis the Menace and a good idea struck her. Alfie had voiced his desire to have a drone like Dennis was using in the episode and Nicole thought it was a wonderful idea. *He wouldn't miss it whilst at school.*

It arrived within days and the detachable super lightweight high-definition camera couldn't have weighed more than 30 grams but reduced the flight time of the drone to around eight minutes. This was not long. Nicole would have to be close by. A little too close by.

In the intervening days, any spare hour was spent parked up on the outskirts of Blacklock Farmland, observing. By undertaking fly-by visual recons of the tractors at work she was able to deduce that Robert and David never worked together, and that Robert favoured the red Kubota and David the green John Deere. *This is good.*

Robert also tended to take himself off to the furthest reaches of their land, leaving David closer to home. They never seemed to speak either.

From the air, Nicole was able to match specific fields with the pre-programmed fields and boundaries in the Command-Center. The advanced guidance technology upgraded in the most recent software update, allowed John Deere to track and automate straight-track guidance modes and auto-turn facilities. Plotting this meant that Nicole could surmise which field was scheduled for which day. She was ready for a dry run.

That morning she dropped Alfie off at school early. She'd paid for the breakfast club for a couple of weeks under the pretence of some early morning appointments she was having and made sure there was no particular day that could be singled out for her clandestine activity.

She dropped him off at 7 am and headed to her usual parking spot. She was about to pull off the road and tuck herself behind a thick hedge when she saw a flash of red on the left of her

30

peripheral vision. Filled with sudden alarm, she aborted her manoeuvre and rammed her foot onto the accelerator instead. The red tractor filled her rear-view mirror. It was following her along this country road and its sudden appearance had caused her heart rate to increase dramatically. She was fixated on Robert, who she could just make out in her mirrors, bobbing up and down with the seat suspension. She became aware of something in front of her and her eyes snapped back to the road ahead to notice the road's sharp bend as she almost ploughed straight into an ancient walnut tree. She reacted quickly though, managing to scandi-flick her black hatchback around the bend. She was loaded with anxiety; this was drawing far too much attention to herself. This was not good.

She dropped a gear and sped off. She'd become very familiar with this route and shaved the corners off wherever she could to put as much distance between her and Robert Lock. She didn't like this feeling; she didn't like being seen. What if she'd had an accident at that moment and he had recognised her from the previous week? It was too much to bear. She rounded a few more bends and came out a couple of miles down Station Road. She turned left and headed back towards town.

Nicole felt calmer now and glanced at the drone sitting in the footwell of the passenger seat. Then she looked back up to the road ahead. The left turn she took not ten minutes ago was coming up. She sighed. *No time like the present.* Despite wanting to just flee home and hide, she reminded herself why this was so important. Alfie. She simply could not let him down.

As Alfie was being let out to play for break, Nicole was carrying his drone through a small wooded area beside the largest of the Lock fields.

It was her own playtime.

WILDFIRE

* * *

She set up her base; her laptop teetered on the side of a fallen tree and the drone sat idle a few metres away beside the field edge. On the walk up from the car she'd considered whether this was necessary now. She'd already witnessed Robert in the red Kubota this morning, it was highly unlikely he'd have switched vehicles in the past half hour. In her professional career she wouldn't have been the one to make this call. She would have been instructed to proceed without knowing with absolutely certainty that the right mark was in the vehicle. She would have presumed that the control room had either verified it themselves already, or that the possible collateral damage didn't outweigh the opportunity.

Regardless, she wasn't going to make any mistakes. If this was the real thing then she'd need to go through these steps and she'd much rather do that now, than on the day.

It was quite a windy day: 21 mph winds from the southeast. Not ideal for drone flying, but needs must. She remote dialled into the Lock's CommandCenter interface and opened the scheduled job. It showed as *In Progress*. The dashboard gave a percentage complete gauge showing 13% done.

Without looking up she picked up the control pad for the drone and it hummed to life, kicking up loose ground as it nimbly zipped up into the sky. It was a marvel really, these drones, how easy they must make recon these days. She wondered how far the agency deployment had gone. *Bet they use them all the time.*

The video stream appeared on her screen; she could plainly see Lock's progress as the bottom strip of field was a dark, rich brown of freshly tilled earth, leaving the rest a murky grey of hard, compacted dirt. Almost at the end of a line, she saw the unmistakable green of the John Deere—its bright yellow wheels and the rotavator's bright orange livery the only discernible colour in the image. She navigated the drone to hover directly over the tractor, out of sight, then slowly dropped the altitude and began to drift left. From here Nicole could also assess the rotavator blades. The bright orange tool was attached to the rear of the machine and consisted of a wide slab of orange metal, like a flap running the full width of the machine. This innocuous flap belied the formidable blades thereunder. Rotating at speed, the angled black teeth were a blur of activity.

She knew from previous passes that Lock would allow the tractor to self-drive the line and would turn in his seat to frequently look out of the back window of the cab at his progress. He always turned to his right, meaning a recce from the left-hand side of the vehicle should go unnoticed.

Nicole manoeuvred the drone to get a clearer view of the cab, dropping it to within three metres of the cab roof and maintaining a forward trajectory. It was him. She was completely sure of that. It was definitely David Lock driving—his paunchy belly clear as day through the window, straining against his mud-green body warmer.

He turned in his seat at that moment, startling Nicole and she pushed the joystick upwards with a start, avoiding detection. But a gust of wind at that moment thrust the drone leftwards, leaving the tractor behind to turn for the next run, as the drone landed in the branches of an old horse chestnut tree by the side of the field. *Shit.* She tried to keep her cool. The video stream showed that the tractor was still moving away, unaware. *Good.* It also showed that the ground was a considerable way off. *Shit.*

137

She swivelled the camera around to try and gauge the extent of the entanglement. It barely looked stuck at all from this angle but it wasn't budging. She tried to get the drone to pull itself free, ramming it up to full power and hoping the force would allow it to break loose. *Nope.*

Nicole took another look towards the tractor, it was nearing the end of its run on the far side. Shortly he'd turn and be back facing the treeline... and the drone. *Shit.*

Nicole tried something different. She slammed the drone controls up, down, up and down, creating a bounce. The feed blurred and made for disorientating viewing, but it was working. At that moment there was a sudden gunshot and a flock of black crows scattered from the woodland at the bottom end of the field, perfectly coinciding with the escaped drone. She couldn't believe her luck. She flew the drone back to her position as fast as she could. Back on the ground she swiftly picked it up and collapsed its arms, heart racing, and returned to her laptop.

She just wanted to get the hell out of there. The dry run was successful, even though she'd had a run-in with Robert and got the bloody drone stuck. But the outcome was the same: she had correctly identified the field and the farmer. She had to calm herself though and test one last element. She patched into his in-vehicle computer and sent through an error code—a code which stopped the rotating blades dead. She watched from the treeline as Lock extracted himself begrudgingly from the cab and went to the rear of the tractor to investigate. Just as he bent to take a look, she cancelled the error and the rotating blades erupted back into life. David Lock hobbled quickly back to the cab to continue his task.

30

* * *

That night she had that feeling again—where she felt minuscule. She could visualise the edges of the room moving rapidly away from her as she shrunk smaller and smaller, the items of furniture receding into the edges of the room.

She felt insignificant. Lonely.

She felt lost.

31

That day started the same as every other. The alarm sounded and cut through the heady, thick air in the cramped bedroom. David Lock roused himself as best he could. His head was heavy from last night's drinking. And yesterday afternoon's drinking. And yesterday morning's drinking. He sniffed in hard, the mucus caught in this throat and made him gag. The stench of stale alcohol lingered in the air and the rising nausea hit hard.

He stumbled to the bathroom and tried to suck in cleaner air to feel normal again. *What's normal? Not this...* Desperate for a piss, he braced himself against the wall with his left arm, elbow locked, he rested his forehead against his bicep and struggled to get his right hand to work. He got most of it in the bowl. Swaying terribly he looked down at his own dick to shake the last drops away and realised he'd slept in his clothes again. Like he gave a shit.

He trudged heavily back into the bedroom searching for something, something important. Lock pushed an old porn mag onto the bare floor and uncovered a half-empty bottle of Jack. He swigged a mouthful, careful not to swallow it right away. He swilled it around his teeth, allowing the warm liquid to reach every millimetre of his mouth and take some of the slimy stale coating with it. He swallowed hard and grimaced.

31

Pulling on his knackered boots, he headed out onto the landing. He could already smell bacon and it made him feel worse. He could sense Rob within, before he even got close. *Fucking hell.* Trying not to think too much about the possible interactions he could have with his older brother, David let out a faltering, deep sigh and lumbered into the intolerable heat. It was the only heated room in the house and only because of the Aga on constant vigil.

David said nothing as he entered, and headed straight for the back door. Rebel, the Dutch Shepherd, otherwise at ease under the kitchen table at Robert's feet, had expectantly raised herself to greet her favourite. He ignored her doe eyes.

"Marnin'," mumbled Robert, looking up from the paperwork splayed across the table and holding a bacon sandwich halfway to his mouth.

David grunted a reply, ignoring the dog's expectant face. Robert couldn't make out what the grunt meant, so carried on.

"You dern the regent field a'day?"

"Yup, but tha' bludy row'to'vater kip cuttin' oot. Piece'a shite." David's hand had made it to the door handle.

Robert didn't reply. His opinion was unwavering—it was less likely the equipment at fault and more likely his drunkard of a brother doing something wrong. But he knew when to speak up and when to let things lie. This was one of those times. *Jeez he stinks.*

David left the house without exchanging another word and headed across to the barn to get the new John Deere out. Although the JD was the new purchase, Robert had allowed his brother to adopt it as his preferred vehicle purely down to the fact that the majority of the driving was done automatically.

As Robert had scheduled in all the jobs, he made sure that job-to-job movement avoided any and all public highways. David might be drunk most of the time but he wasn't stupid, he knew what his brother was doing and he resented him for it. Trying to control him like that, as if he was still a boy. He hated him. "Why dunt he just fall down dead, the good-fer-nuttin' bastard and leave me be?"

David climbed the steps into the cab, his head pounding. He'd forgotten to take some paracetamol for this headache *because of that bastard*. The engine rumbled into life and he made his way out of the farmyard and through the back gate. The dazzling orange rotavator still connected to the rear hitch, bouncing along with the tractor suspension.

The Regent's Field was their second largest field and because of its position and natural irrigation, always gave them the best yield of beet. As he ambled along the track, Lock selected the pre-programmed job from the menu on his dashboard and let the GPS locate the vehicle.

He reached down into the footwell to the left of the steering column and lifted up another bottle of Jack. He needed to stop feeling sick. He took a couple of swigs. He was at the edge of Regent's now and guided the John Deere through the gap in the hedge, frightening away a few small birds from their peaceful morning routine.

He swung the great machine around to get it into position. His mind was foggy for sure, but getting a tractor in the right place was a skill he'd learnt almost before he could walk. He lowered the hydraulics and let the blades of the rotavator rest on the hard ground. He then initiated the programme and the tractor lurched into forward motion. Lock continued to swig his bottle between turns, allowing the tractor to do the hard

31

work. The nausea had all but gone and Lock once again found solace in his tranquil isolation.

About an hour into the job, the tractor abruptly stopped. Lock looked at the dashboard screen and swore. A familiar error message had pinged up to say that there was an obstruction affecting the PTO stub. The Power Take-Off stub was what transferred power from the tractor to whatever its attached to. Lock huffed.

"For fuck's sake."

He chucked the bottle into the foot-well, dismounted from the cab and walked around to the rear. The protective flap covering the rotating teeth was still open. The hydraulic arms that controlled the incline was supposed to close when the machine shut down or stopped—for obvious safety reasons. Lock didn't pay it any mind, he carried on being angry at the machinery, angry at his life.

He stooped down to try and see better, but the pressure in his head sky-rocketed and the queasiness returned. He straightened up and closed his eyes, waiting for the sensation to pass. There was a lull in the wind at that moment and he thought he could detect a strange sound. He squinted involuntarily as he looked up and about, trying to locate the noise. He couldn't. His focus was back on the tractor now.

He stepped over one of the three-point hitch arms to get close enough to the PTO stub to investigate better but he still couldn't see anything. At that moment he heard a whirring sound again. This one, however, was different—it was like a grinding whine from brakes being held on... but only just. A nanosecond later the rotating teeth of the rotavator shuddered back into action. The blades were so close to the back of Lock's legs he almost fell backwards onto them, but managed to keep upright.

The danger he was in hadn't really registered through his Jack-riddled foggy brain. He never would have supposed the tractor would move of its own accord. But it did—just a couple of inches. The teeth caught the back of his right trouser leg and he screamed out in pain and crashed his knees down onto the metal framework in front of him. The pain searing through his body and into his brain was immense. He could scarcely breathe. The tractor moved again—a sudden lurch forward another few inches. His knees fell to the ground. He didn't think he could feel more pain than he already did, but he was wrong. Both lower legs were getting repeatedly mangled by the blades and he grabbed at the dirt trying desperately to claw his way forward and out of harm's way, but no matter how much progress he thought he'd made, the tractor stayed with him.

One last jolt forward from the John Deere was all he now needed. The unapologetic black, angled teeth got a final hold on the soft flesh at the back of Lock's leg and instead of ripping the flesh, it pulled him in.

The briefest of howls and he was gone. Just a mangled mess of blood-soaked torn fabric, bone and unrecognisable body parts. The tractor came to a halt and everything slowed to a final stop.

There was a moment of silence and then the gentle early-morning sounds of the birdlife started up once more.

And the low hum of a drone drifted away, leaving the crows to descend on the remains of David Terrence Lock.

32

The local press went berserk.

This was a wonderfully delicious story of a drunken blight on the town being poetically mangled by his own farming equipment in what was one of the most horrific farming accidents the county had ever seen. The industry news sites and social media lapped it up. The rival Midrakes were quoted in every publication they could get into, damning the younger brother and painting a very black image of the only surviving Lock family member.

March moved into April but still the news outlets peddled the story, using Lock as the martyr to address industry-wide concerns over the inherent dangers of agricultural farming. The Health and Safety Executive twittered on with its assertion that one person a week dies in farming-related incidents. But they weren't going to be leading *this* investigation—which was fortuitous for Nicole. The Work-Related Death Protocol principles meant that the police were taking the lead on this one.

Local officers were already predisposed against the Lock family it seemed, so their remit was less about the farming legislation and more about culpability. Nicole kept a close eye on the police developments behind the scenes and was relieved to read the reports: Lock should not have been standing where he was. Furthermore, they could not fathom why he had stood there at all whilst the machinery was in operation. However, there were no signs of any interference from outside forces. David Lock became another fatality statistic linked to excessive alcohol consumption.

The farming industry magazines defended Lock, citing his connections with Young Farmers and British Sugar. They took a more sympathetic view against his failings and instead considered whether the stresses and strains upon agricultural farmers was in fact the root cause of this terrible accident, and that perhaps more needed to be done to address and improve the mental health of farmers young and old. Others addressed the call for more rigorous legislation around operating heavy machinery when intoxicated, regardless of whether it's on private land, and spouted old adages about a man's domain.

Despite the successful outcome, Nicole had started to spiral.

She was desperately trying to display an air of normality whenever Alfie was around—and she thought she was succeeding—but whenever he was at school, she fell apart.

She still wasn't sleeping at night and she'd had to reduce her hours at the library for fear of getting dismissed altogether. She lay on the sofa now. The post-lunch food coma was kicking in and she'd made the mistake of putting 'Dickinson's Real Deal' on the telly. She couldn't keep her eyes open.

The discussions on the TV were wafting into her subconscious and her thoughts morphed into a swirl of confused, overlapping images. She could picture the artefacts being described by David Dickinson, his pinstripe dark suit dancing in front of her eyes but with no face, just two dark bushy brows crowned with a white, blow-dried bouffant. He was no longer cradling a 15th century snuff box carved from Indian rosewood and once owned by Lady Wotsitnoodle, but a plum-coloured velvet jewellery box. She'd seen this box before and it was making her feel anxious. *Why is David Dickinson holding my box? Where did he...? What is it worth at today's auction?*

Tears silently rolled down her cheeks but she didn't wake. David's suit and hair were now drifting though a hallway. It was lavish and shiny and she was following him. It was gold and expensive, tacky in her opinion, but she'd never tell the owner. David rounded the corner to the stairs but she didn't follow. She turned left and approached a pair of heavy, carved doors. The right one was slightly ajar and she walked silently across the tiled floor until she was inches from it. There were voices. She could hear the voices—they were raised, shouting at one another. No—only one voice was shouting. The other voice only occasionally hazarding a response. There was so much anger.

"...OUT OF YOUR FUCKING MIND? Do you seriously think I would have shared *anything* with that bitch if I'd have known the truth?"

"No Sir, I di—" the second man was interrupted.

"You find that worthless cunt and you bring her to *me*. Do you think you can manage that?"

Before waiting for a reply, "For fuck's sake, you lot are fucking useless. HOW COULD YOU LET THIS HAPPEN? I'll sort it myself."

Instinctively, she knew he was talking about her. She should run. She needed to get out. She couldn't remember who was behind the door but she knew what they were capable of. She could remember sitting idle, spectating, as this man had done hateful, gruesome things to people who had wronged him—or to those he'd only *thought* had wronged him, or just looked at him funny. She was in too deep.

She'd wheedled her way into his life to assess the position and locate the evidence her employer needed, but the deeper she got, the more they wanted from her. It had become too much. There were too many liberties being exploited and they weren't getting her out. They had let her down. And now she was having to take risks—risks she should avoid at all costs—but she couldn't see another way out. But now they'd caught her. Someone had found out about her real identity, her real reason for being there. What's more, this man was beyond furious about it. The betrayal, the insult.

Who gave a shit if he held the key to global cyberwarfare. Was it worth *this?* Was it really worth her life?

She took a step back from the carved door as it violently crashed back on its hinges, taking a divot out of the console table beside her. A man marched past—not even seeing her—with fire in his eyes and veins throbbing with malice and fury. A few other men trotted along behind him as he stalked off in the direction of the stairs.

Nicole followed. David Dickinson was back, beside her now. "It's priceless." He was gliding along towards the angry party, accompanying her. There were shouts and screams from the landing ahead. They sounded familiar. It was *her* voice. Begging him to stop. The other men had halted halfway up the curved stairs, clearly hesitant at getting too close to the altercation happening above them, but also too nervous to retreat.

Nicole and David moved through them and arrived at the top. This was so familiar, yet so alien to her. She knew where to go and what was happening behind those closed doors without

32

needing to be in earshot. Unbidden, she moved closer still—the voices from within becoming clearer with proximity.

"... me who you're working for, you disgusting bitch," he spat the words out, inches from her face. There was a struggle, the hairs on the back of her head stinging as they were ripped out. Her body was being bruised, hit repeatedly. The side of her head was slammed against the bedframe and her body went limp. It wasn't her body. Was she out here with David? Or in there with... the name wasn't coming to her.

But she knew her body—the body *in there*—was being hurt. Her clothes were ripped off her as she lay semi-conscious, and now semi-naked, on the garish rug beside the bed.

"You're going to tell me *everything...*" The man was demanding so much of her. He was unbuckling his belt. *Was it worth it? Had it been worth it?* The belt was round her neck now and he was forcing her legs apart. The tan leather creaked. More pain, new pain, shot through her body—she was crying. Large tears streamed down her face. She looked back towards the stairs and the men there were tentatively retreating, leaving the other Nicole to her fate. She wasn't Nicole back then.

A few minutes of this limbo went by. The doors flew open and Dickinson scarpered. This other man, this huge, grotesque hulk of a man, sweaty with exertion, anger and power, thundered across to the stairs. His hand grasping a handful of hair and dragging the half-naked woman along the slippery floor with ease. He braced himself at the top of the stairs and flung Sophie down them.

Darkness.

33

Nicole fell from the sofa—her face soaked with tears and sweat. *That was me. The old me. Sophie.* She felt the sensations and pain anew. The turmoil of emotion was agonising. That horrific act from him had resulted in Alfie. She knew that. She had come to terms with that many years ago. She could separate the two versions of herself. She could compartmentalise it all.

But all that hard work with her many, many therapy sessions was beginning to unravel and it was terrifying. She needed to get a handle on this—needed to pick up that healing process again as fast as she could and stop it from getting worse. *No good will come of this.*

A low, intermittent, humming buzz from her phone sounded a million miles away at that moment. But it didn't stop, and seemingly, each vibration brought her closer to reality. Eventually, she glanced down and reached for the handset on the floor beside her. It was Dorothy, the library manager. She swiped at the moisture on her face with one arm, as she raised the phone to her ear with the other.

"Hello Dorothy," she greeted the caller with little strength in her voice.

"Oh goodness, Nic, you sound strange. Are you okay?" Dorothy genuinely did sound concerned for Nicole in that moment and she felt sheepish. She sat herself up more and tried to inject some pep into her reply.

"Oh yeah, yeah, don't worry about me—I'm alright. What can I do for you?"

"Ah well, I know it's your day off and all, but I was wondering if you could cover Sarah's shift this afternoon? I'm in a right pickle about it. She's dislocated a rib—whatever that means—and I have a scheduled scan at the hospital. You wouldn't be able to help me out would you?"

Nicole really needed to keep Dorothy on-side.

"Yeah, I should be able to. I'll have to bring Alfie though."

"That's fine my woman, not a problem."

"Okay, I'll grab him from school at 3:15 and be there straight after?"

"That's perfect. See you then. Thank you!"

"K. Bye."

Nicole peeled herself up off the floor and made her way upstairs to freshen up. She didn't have long before she needed to leave anyway. She straightened out her hair and gave her face a quick wash.

Compartmentalise Nicole. You've got this.

* * *

The rest of the afternoon was uneventful. Alfie was good as gold, sitting in the kid's section and systematically going through all the lift-the-flap books. Nicole was in a bit of a daze but doing okay considering.

No one asked her anything. There were no issues with

the self-serve machines. No printer jams. Nothing. It was lovely. The last patron left at 7:02 pm and that was when Alfie materialised complaining he was hungry. Nicole collected up her bags and Alfie's school bookbag as he pulled on his coat and they discussed the possibility of stopping in for Fish n' Chips. Alfie was jumping about in excited anticipation of the carb-fest, when Nicole realised that one of the fabric tote bags she'd collected up with her own didn't belong to her. It was a similar size and colour, but definitely not hers. She looked inside to find the answer and nearly dropped the lot.

Inside the tote were three books and she could already see familiar makeshift bookmarks peeking out of the tops of all three. Her stomach lurched.

Alfie was pestering her to get going now. She didn't have time to think about this. She just shook away the feeling and carried them off, vowing to tackle this once and for all later.

Her stomach was rumbling too and the smell from across the road was torture.

34

Nicole needed to get through this.

She knew she had to get through this. She couldn't fail. She couldn't just curl up into a ball and ignore everything, despite wanting to. She had to carry on.

The same feeling had swarmed her after the birth of Alfie. Up to that point she had resigned herself to a life of pain and anguish, paranoia and fear. But when she saw his tiny mushed-up creased face, merely four seconds old, she had snapped out of it almost instantaneously. The strong-willed, tenacious and resourceful Nicole had returned. She was invigorated, reborn. All the words of her therapist suddenly made sense and she could see a path through—a path to a brighter world, with no more lies and no more fear.

It had worked as well. For five years she had overcome all that she'd previously had to endure—the weeks of torture and torment—but she was dangerously close to losing her faculties again.

What she really wanted, was to revisit her therapist. Gail Pemberton knew everything about everything and all Nicole wanted was to speak to her again and not have to revisit and retell all that had happened. But Gail Pemberton wasn't a regular therapist. She was employed through the agency Nicole used to work for and any contact with her would be akin to dancing around outside the offices with a neon sign and a death wish.

Nicole considered for a moment whether she could start the whole process again with a new therapist, but there was so much that she'd have to redact it hardly seemed worth it. What help could she really get if she couldn't even be honest about the events that led her there?

No, the only thing she could conceivably do was to go it alone. Nicole decided to risk detection and break into the servers at the agency. She'd helped to build them, so she knew how best to get in—unless they'd changed something fundamental. But once in she could locate her records—all her therapist notes and reports would be in her records; she could read them through herself and use them to remember her therapist's words and techniques. It was the only thing she could think of to do.

And whilst that was going on, she had been all but *handed* another three library books. The server break-in was yet again shelved for another day.

The other books that led her to Wolston and Lock were stacked up in the back corner of her wardrobe, hidden behind the few dresses and coats she owned but never wore. These clothes were too jolly for her right now—drew too much attention—so they hung here instead, hiding the library books that she had purposefully removed from circulation on the library computer system.

But these three new ones couldn't be ignored—not even for a short while. The pain and fear, the suffering, was once again becoming so fresh in her mind that now, more than ever before, she felt the desire to keep Alfie from being anywhere near that man. *What was his name? Why can't I remember?*

34

The tote bag was a thicker one than her own—expensive linen. The internal tag had been removed and she could see the frayed threads where it had once been. The handles were proper cotton webbing straps, not just fabric like the cheaper ones. The main body of the bag was plain, a natural light beige colour, matching the handles. Nothing on it at all. Nothing to give away where it might have come from.

Her shoulders began to sag.

Without much enthusiasm, she reached in and pulled out the books. As she'd seen before, there were three. Pieces of yellow paper peeped out from the tops of each one. She held the first up—the smallest, so naturally the one that sat on top: *Little Women* by Louisa M. Alcott. The book felt light and dainty in her hands. The cover depicted the four March sisters at leisure, outdoors under the shade of a large tree. Nicole remembered reading it as a young girl and knew that this book only covered half of the well-known movie version. This was only half the story. She didn't know whether that fact was relevant but noted it nonetheless.

The paper slip was tucked in near the back: page 210. This was halfway through the very last chapter of the book. Nicole skim-read it now. The family were all together again but Jo was fretting about the possibility of her older sister Meg's possible betrothal to Mr Brooke, frightened he'd be taking away her best friend. The stately intrusion of their Aunt March turned Meg's hesitation into surety; the pair were engaged. And there the story ends.

Placing *Little Women* beside the bag, she reached for the next book. This one larger, thicker and all green. A plump robin perched on an old gate key. *The Secret Garden* by Frances Hodgson Burnett. Nicole had never read this book, nor seen a movie of it, although she was aware they did exist.

The ominous yellow slip was tucked into the front of this one—right on the first chapter. The story introduction set the scene of a young girl arriving at a manor house to live with her uncle and being generally regarded as a spoilt, sour-faced, disagreeable child.

Nicole covered the March sisters with the fat robin and moved on.

The last book wasn't one Nicole was familiar with at all. At first glance, it made her think of those tacky romance novels that live on a rotating stand in the library, apologetically tucked away beside the photocopier. This cover was a mid-blue, blending into the image of an elegant garden housing a quaint white gazebo beside a serene lake, with willow tree fronds reaching down to the water. The white serif typeface, all in capitals, dated the book some twenty years. The author's name rang a bell though—Julia Quinn. Nicole had heard that name recently.

The Viscount Who Loved Me. Reading the blurb gave her the connection: Bridgerton. This was the second in the Bridgerton series of books. *Of course,* she thought. *This must have been the original cover design.* This book cover felt at odds with the content she knew from the TV series. The slip of yellow was blank but tucked in between pages four and five. Nicole read the whole prologue, giving her context for the marker.

It followed the untimely death of the Bridgerton father. It seemed he was fatally allergic to a bee sting. Anthony Bridgerton learns he died of anaphylaxis on page five.

A hot wave of emotion bubbled up from somewhere deep within Nicole. *Where is this going to end? How is it going to end? Will it ever end?* An impending sense of doom was making itself

34

comfortable just behind the right-hand side of her ribcage. She'd had this feeling before and it took months of hard work to rid herself of it.

This can't be happening again.

35

"How about you just help me through the door, eh little man?" Nicole was demonstrating a key motherhood skill—carrying 27 objects of varying size whilst still having a hand free in order to unlock the front door. It was raining, which wasn't helping.

They stepped through the doorway and dried their shoes on April's edition of *Only Twynesham*, as well as three white envelopes of differing sizes, all complete with wet footprints.

"Alfie," Nicole called to him, her tone clearly beckoning him back. "Your shoes don't live there do they?" Nicole indicated the middle of the hallway floor.

Alfie smiled coyly as he walked back to her and did as he was bid, all the while meeting her glare. She couldn't hold the stern look for long though and they were both laughing together as Alfie ran off upstairs to take off his uniform and Nicole collected the trampled post from the mat.

The front page of *Only Twynesham* sported a close up of another pest—this time a hornet. Nicole read about the hornets' nest found in a hollowed-out tree in the woods of the Limeworth estate. They had attacked a woman and her dog; the dog hadn't made it. The venomous flying hornets were not to be trifled with and a stark warning was given to stay away from that area of the woodland.

35

"MUMMY!" Alfie yelled from the top of the stairs.

Nicole walked back out of the kitchen towards the foot of the stairs, "Ye—"

"MUMMY!"

"I'm right here Alfie, you don't need to shout! What is it?"

"There's something weird in my room."

"Wh..." Nicole's brow furrowed and she raced up the stairs two at a time. "What's weird? What is it?"

She met Alfie at the top step as he was pointing towards his open bedroom door. He didn't answer her. She walked past him and entered the room. *Surely no one got in this time, they couldn't have.*

"I can't see anything weird Alfie, if you kept your room ti—"

"ATTACK!"

Alfie ran at her full pelt and knocked her sideways. *An ambush!* Nicole tried to protect herself but it was no use, she was on the floor, Alfie was using her torso as a trampoline and exclaiming that she had to surrender or else. Nicole had whipped off her glasses in a futile attempt at keeping them from getting damaged. Alfie was smiling, and so was she at first. But then she felt the blackness take hold. She felt weak and vulnerable. She was under attack. The smile faded and she felt scared.

"Please Alfie, let me get up, let me—"

"NEVER! You are my prisoner!" Alfie was wielding his pirate sword now and Nicole's chest felt tighter. The walls of his measly bedroom turned dark in her eyes and began to close in on her. She scrabbled about to get on all fours. She wasn't thinking about Alfie now; she just needed to get up.

She crawled to the door, sucking in lungfuls of air. Alfie had climbed onto her back now—it was all a game to him. *He has no idea.*

She righted herself and Alfie fell off, proclaiming his annoyance at her reluctance to play. Nicole mumbled something about needing to go downstairs and walked away from him. He was disappointed, but he'd get over it and forget. Nicole felt overwhelming sadness.

She was back down in the kitchen now, leaning heavily on the tabletop, head bowed. She stayed that way for a while and waited for the emotion to pass. *This is getting tiresome. I can't keep on like this.*

With renewed determination, she pulled out a chair and sat at the table to revisit her notes on this unsuspecting person. All the labour-intensive work had been done already, now it was a matter of tweaking some keywords and metadata to look for someone new. Person number three.

* * *

By the time Alfie's tea was ready, she'd found a potential match. A man by the name of Lawrence Rackham-Hush. He was listed as Deputy Headmaster of Mistlewaite Grange, an illustrious public school on the northern fringes of town. They claimed they were nearer to the grander Falke, but really they were in the boundary of middling Twynesham. The house in *The Secret Garden* was the match here, barely scraping through the algorithm, but results are results. The manor in the book was called Misselthwaite. Close enough. Lawrence Rackham-Hush lived with his wife in a place called Brook House in the oldest part of Twynesham, closest to the church. This was the strongest link—Brooke from *Little Women*. It was a secondary search of his name and previous addresses in Surrey that sealed it though.

Nicole had found old newspaper articles from forty years ago detailing the near-fatal attack on a small four-year-old boy in the village of Dulton-Gissing. He'd been swarmed by wasps at the end of that summer and had experienced a severe reaction to the 86 stings he'd suffered. The young lad was named Larry Rackham then, but the school photo pictured in the newspapers was undoubtedly the same person featured on the *Meet the faculty* page of Mistlewaite Grange's website. His hooked nose and close-set eyes were easily distinguishable.

Further searches for Larry/Lawrence Rackham/Rackham-Hush were also very fruitful. Thirty years on from those news articles, there were a flurry of others. They followed the suspension of a history teacher—an Archie Rackham—teaching at a school in Crawley. There were allegations; no charges, no convictions. But allegations. Allegations of improper behaviour whilst in employment there plus the mention of suspension.

Nicole followed the breadcrumbs.

A couple of years after that, Lawrence Rackham had married Helena Edith Hush and Lawrence Archibald Rackham-Hush began life as a teacher of history and latin at Mistlewaite. All previous allegations were seemingly forgotten, or had failed to follow him all the way from West Sussex. And he had been teaching there since.

School records were horrendously protected in these public schools. Nicole pondered on this: the more wealthy these old establishments were the more arrogant, making tight-fisted, mean decisions when security was on the table. As such, it wasn't hard to get into the servers at Mistlewaite.

They weren't terribly well organised though. Nicole would have assumed such well-educated people would employ good naming conventions, but it wasn't to be. It took longer than it had any cause to be, but Nicole eventually located the personnel records and found one labelled LRH.

LRH's file contained the standard fare, with a notable absence of any complaints. Nicole hadn't been expecting this. She'd expected to find *something*, even if it was one report of some entitled toff whose mummy and daddy were upset about detention or something. But the absence of anything at all didn't stack up.

Nicole's interest piqued at this, so she went digging.

In a deleted cache of files spanning a decade, she found dozens of documents. Page upon page of minor reports, complaints and allegations from students current and former. Spanning years. Dirty Larry wasn't just the history and latin teacher, he also took PE. His only qualification here appeared to be that he was the youngest member of the teaching staff. *Maybe he was the only one without arthritis.* PE classes involved communal showers and open-plan changing rooms. The pages went on. The more she searched for them in this cache, the more she found. They were reasonably well buried and for all intents and purposes *deleted*—at least that's what Larry must have thought.

But these things have a way of finding you again.

36

Okay, this is all getting a bit out of control now. I'm losing the plot and need to get a grip. Alfie is going to start getting affected by this soon—if he's not already. And that is something I'm not happy about.

Nicole had begun to obsess. Things were getting too much. There were too many plates spinning and something was going to fall and smash if Nicole didn't get her shit together soon. Someone knew her history, knew her previous life, and was threatening to expose the existence of Alfie to his father—the father being an awful human being who would undoubtedly come for them both if he found out. And only one of them would live through the experience.

That someone was using this as leverage to get her to enact some sort of weird vigilante vendetta against atrocious locals. Granted, these horrid people should be stopped, but this—even with Nicole's currently skewed moral compass—wasn't the way to go about it.

Nicole needed to revisit her previous life and address this head-on.

She would never find a way out otherwise.

Larry and her blackmailer would need to be shelved, just for a while. Nicole felt the mounting pressure to get her therapy records again, it was all she could think about. There was nothing to be done until then.

37

Nicole attempted to hack in to the agency servers. As expected, it wasn't easy. Protocols and security encryption tiers *had* been altered since her time there and it took cunning and more of a concerted effort than she'd bargained for to get through.

But get through she did.

She located her personnel file in an archived server, seemingly housing nothing but the records of those now decommissioned, retired or deceased. She mused that at least she fell into bucket number one.

Her file was protected—perhaps they all were—but the challenge of this last gateway was merely a pothole to Nicole and her superior ability. She was able to copy the contents of the file onto her laptop and back out of the hack, covering her tracks as she retreated. She was careful, but out of everyone whose file she'd broken into recently, this bunch were the most likely to catch her. They knew exactly what to look for—she'd probably trained the buggers.

The file was in her old name—actually the name before the last old name—Sophie Baxter. The first document was a summary of employment: dates, positions, salaries and the like; known aliases and which operations they had been used for; known associates and connections outside of the agency.

Alfie's old name was there. Underneath it the words: *Steen J Marlowe (Father) - Operation Hummingbird.*

The room around Nicole began to spin. Her vision narrowed—all her periphery pixelated and the square inch of screen where these words now sat was all she could see. The blackness around her closed in and great pressure built up in her forehead and behind her eyes. She closed them against the dark tide and tried to get a hold on her heart rate and breathing. *You know how to stop this. Breathe. Calm.* The pressure waned, and as it did so, the memories previously forgotten took its place—memories that she'd repressed—things she'd deliberately hidden and stored away. It had all started to come back.

Her vision restored, she searched for *Hummingbird* further in her files. There was a dossier with this title. She opened it. As she read on, it all flooded back. She felt such empowerment at having this knowledge now. Before, it had been a terrible burden, painful to keep, but now—with this happening to Sophie, a different person altogether—she, Nicole, could *use* it. It gave her answers. It gave her leads.

Operation Hummingbird had begun two years prior to Alfie's birth. There was intelligence that a wealthy Scandinavian-Brit was dealing arms overseas close to the Russian border, but that the business was branching out into cyberwarfare. The compound this Steen Marlowe had built for himself was state of the art and riddled with all manner of encrypted door entry codes and security protocols. The guy was insanely paranoid and the agency needed eyes on. The agency—an undocumented branch of MI6—was a governmental agency that very few people knew existed. They insisted that the agent deployed would need to surpass Marlowe's ability in order to find out

37

what his cyberwarfare capabilities were in order to fight it. This is where Sophie came into the narrative.

She'd been working in mission control up to that point—poached from MI5, who'd poached her from GCHQ. Out of everyone, she was the one they selected. She'd had field training previously and had shown real promise, now she was put through a rigorous physical training programme. Sophie had loved it. She was young and ambitious, bright and wanted the challenge. She'd felt strong. Invulnerable.

She closed her eyes for a moment and recalled that time. She could picture so much of it now—she could walk herself around in these different scenes, see the people there and remember who they all were.

She returned to the report. Page after page of code made up the bulk of the first file. It was the programme she'd uncovered after infiltrating the compound several months before. The agency had found an opening for her in the guise of a job advert—of sorts.

There had been intimations on the dark web that this Marlowe needed a world-class hacker to stress-test a worm programme. She was the perfect candidate. It definitely didn't hurt that she was a fit young woman either.

She recalled sitting at a desk in a safe house above an old theatre on Drury Lane, with just a laptop and phone. She'd written a short worm code and broken through Marlowe's first defences within the hour. The worm had started to infect his systems, one by one, moving from terminal to terminal. The code had her phone number embedded in it—everywhere.

Her phone had rung within the minute. It was him. His deep, resonant voice had been trying to sound calm and she could tell he was impressed, but he had not been able to disguise his fearfulness. She had stopped the worm when he offered her the job. She was in.

It turned out he had wanted to get her on-site at an associate's palatial home during a dinner party, inserting a worm and destroying his business. This target's recent business transactions had been encroaching on Marlowe's territory and he didn't like vying for contracts. This was why Marlowe couldn't do it himself, despite having some skill.

He had liked Sophie so much he'd kept her there, improving his own security measures. Before long, she'd been a trusted associate and he had brought her into the fold. She'd learned practically everything about his big scheme—a scheme to infiltrate, infect and systematically hold to ransom entire governments. He called it *Wildfire*. She'd reported back as soon as she'd dared, assuming that she'd be extracted, hailed a hero and leading the team to combat the threat.

But that's not what happened.

She had been too valuable where she was, they said. They had kept her in. They even wanted more. They wanted her to infiltrate and sabotage the threat from the inside—alone. She'd not believed it at first. She assumed they would come and get her. But it didn't happen. Weeks went by before she accepted that they had no intention of pulling her out at all. She had been devastated. Recalling all this, the hot swell of betrayal bubbled up at the memory. *How dare they! Those fucking entitled...*

She remembered it all so clearly. The desperation and panic she'd felt and the chronic loneliness. She'd been on ops before but nothing like this, and never *completely* alone like this. She had been only twenty-seven.

She began to relive the events of that fateful day. Her desperation had caused her to get sloppy and careless. She hadn't covered her tracks as well as she should have and her regular cries for help to the agency required regular communications that she shouldn't have been making at all. She'd exposed herself, and they'd caught her.

The attack in her room that day was brutal. She'd never been hurt like that before and it was severely damaging. Her purple velvet jewellery box was standing on the end table beside her bed. It was where she'd hidden physical evidence, such as thumb drives, in a compartment underneath. It was worth a considerable amount to the agency—to the country. And then, protecting it and trying to get it out of there, had cost *her* so much.

She barely remembered falling down the stairs, but she remembered the torture that came after.

She'd been stripped, searched and hosed down out in one of the barns, before being clad in a scratchy green boiler suit. A black hood was rammed down over her face and blacked-out goggles forced over the top, blocking out all light. Bulky headphones were placed on top of it all, filling her head with the loud screams of babies crying and dentists' drills. The sounds made her nerves twitch and her ears whine. She would have sworn her ears bled.

She was mostly sat on the hard floor like this for hours, days. She was constantly watched, endlessly made to hold stress-positions, and never allowed to sag or sleep. Between these sessions were lengthy bouts of questioning. They wanted to know who she worked for, what she was doing there, who she was contacting, and what she'd told them. She had confessed just enough for them to keep her alive. They learnt names and some details, but nothing of real consequence.

In the darkness, on the sixth or seventh day, she was moved

to an empty room. Sophie was thrown in and abandoned.

* * *

Nicole didn't need to keep reading. She knew all this. What she needed to read were the therapist's notes and records. She scrolled through hundreds of pages of transcripts looking for the one session, the session where it had all spilled out. Although the therapist's advice and comfort had fallen on Sophie's deaf ears back then, Nicole was hoping she'd be able to draw in all those words and make use of them now. Arguably, this was when she needed them the most.

But before she got there, she noticed a name scrawled in the bottom right corner of one of the quarterly status updates between her therapist, Gail Pemberton, and Gail's supervisor. Nicole skim-read the page. It was a highlight report of Sophie's progress, a summary of the advice given and a proposal for next steps. *I thought these things were confidential.* Nicole chastised herself for being so naive. *Of course an agency therapist would share—they probably told half my colleagues.*

But the name looked familiar to Nicole. She'd never seen, met or spoken to any other therapist other than Gail, but the name was definitely ringing a tiny bell. Under the scrawl of blue biro, was printed Dr. C Bishop.

Bishop. Bishop? Where have I seen that name?

Nicole searched the scrawl for clues. The first name was a similar length to Bishop, had a descender as the second letter—maybe a "y". *God this handwriting is shit—no wonder it's a Doctor.* The last letter, or letters, were obscured by the ostentatious "B". *Clyde? Cyrilla? Cybil? Cy...*

Nicole was interrupted by the doorbell. Ordinarily, she would have ignored it, but she was waiting for a delivery and didn't want it to end up at one of her neighbours' houses. She loathed having to go round to next-doors'—they had a doorbell cam and she hated it. She needed a break from all this anyway. She took in the parcel but left the door ajar. Slipping on her trainers and pulling on her jacket, she headed out into the spring sunshine for a walk.

She needed to clear her head.

38

Nicole walked fast at first. She needed to expend some of the nervous energy that was coursing through her. The day was mild and she was soon far too warm in her jacket. It was annoying carrying it but what could she do?

She thought about her therapist Gail and the sessions they'd had together. She'd warmed to Gail immensely. It hadn't taken her long to forget that she'd worked for the agency too. Nicole was kicking herself. Despite the gratitude, she also felt like a mug. It was a complex mix of contradicting sensibilities.

Some of Gail's words were finding their way back to her now though. Sophie wouldn't listen at first, but Nicole could. And would. As suggested, Nicole took herself through the events of recent months. No judgements, no detours or scrutiny, or analysis—just relive the events in their proper order, she told herself. Nicole gave in and allowed the memories to find her. She walked away from town, north, alongside the railway track which headed out only to the coast these days, the track south just used as a cycleway.

The open fields and blue skies were a metaphor for her mind—openness and light. She must remember to just be open.

Nicole's thoughts were synchronous with the environment

around her. She covered the events leading up to identifying Wolston before she reached the first rail bridge, the events leading up to her demise before the second. And so it went on until she neared a level crossing. The alarm was pinging and the barriers were slowly descending. Although Nicole could have continued walking alongside the tracks, she paused to watch the train approach.

There was something oddly exhilarating about a speeding train passing through a crossing like this—the threat, the danger, so near and with such minimal protection. Nothing at all preventing someone from getting too close. The vulnerability was palpable. Nicole heard the train draw near. It was coming from the coast towards town, the sun behind her. As she leant on a fence post and waited, she returned to her recollections.

The train was drawing level with the road now, as Nicole's minds-eye drew level with the boy on his scooter and the trailer bearing down on him. The consuming cacophony from the train wheels on the old metal tracks was comforting and served to relieve the incessant screaming of her inner thoughts. She let it consume her. Numb her. The rumbling intensified, the rhythm pounding through her body. Speaking to her. No other sounds could be detected but the shriek of metal on metal, the groan of the carriages, the wooshing of the disturbed air and the hiss from the brakes—the sounds blending into a melody: *hiss screech creak clack, hiss screech creak - hiss... hiss... bish... Bishop.*

"Bishop."

Cynthia Bishop. Mrs Cynthia Bishop. The grandmother. Seven-year-old Alexander Hargreaves' grandmother. The boy killed by David Lock. She had been the one leaving all the books for me. She had been the one to amend that book dedication from "For Kate" to "For Alex".

All of this is for Alex.

Her jaw was slack from disbelief—the sounds from the train made soft from distance. It may as well have hit her—she was floored. All the snippets of memory were awakening and slamming into one another, building a comprehensive picture. She had come across Cynthia Bishop's name before. Dr C Bishop was the person who had co-signed every one of Gail Pemberton's reports.

The more she considered what she knew within the context of the grandmother to Alexander Hargreaves being one and the same as her own therapist's supervisor, it all became logical.

Burying Cynthia's own, personal vengeance within two other murders was decidedly brilliant. She had to admire the woman for her tenacity. Despite all this, there were a lot of unanswered questions. Those would have to wait.

Nicole had lost the capacity to continue her walk and this revelation had also sapped all cognitive strength from her too. She was bewildered and fatigued. She was consumed by an imperative need to hold Alfie. If she headed back now, she'd be ridiculously early for the school pick-up, but that didn't bother her today.

All she could think about was seeing his happy, adoring face and holding him close. *Maybe I'll take him to the park, it's such a nice day for it after all.*

39

On reflection, Nicole could properly comprehend her new found situation. She now possessed knowledge. Knowledge that gave her intelligence. Intelligence that could set her free.

Cynthia Bishop *had* to be the one doing this—it all fitted. She'd been privy to all Nicole's—Sophie's—deepest introspections and ruminations. She would know everything. Everything that Nicole had gone through and how she'd been able to build herself back up again afterwards. Cynthia would also have known about her newly assigned identity, Laura Freeman, and would have had access to follow her progress in that new life—all through Gail Pemberton. Cynthia would have known where Laura and her baby boy were relocated. And she would have also known that Laura continued to experience deep-rooted paranoia that the baby's father would discover the truth and hunt them both down. So much so, that Laura was planning an identity change of her own.

As Laura, Nicole had told Gail things she'd never confessed to anyone. And then Gail had told all to her supervisor. She had no doubt that Gail meant well, it was protocol after all. She had no idea that Cynthia Bishop would use that knowledge somehow—how could she have?

But now Nicole also knew about Lawrence Rackham-Hush.

Larry the nonce. Larry the nonce who had continued to get away with years of abuse to young boys within his care. *Perhaps I'll deal with him anyway. Of all the people that make up society, paedophiles are right up there with the worst of the worst.*

There were a lot of things she wanted, needed, to find out about this Cynthia Bishop. Nicole knew she'd only have one chance to do it and get the answers she required. She needed time to prepare. Time she could have, assuming Cynthia was watching somehow, by continuing in her pursuit against Larry. Cynthia would be none the wiser that whilst she observed Nicole's progress towards ridding the world of Larry, she'd be the object of scrutiny herself.

Nicole needed to tread very carefully.

She mustn't misstep.

* * *

Later that week Nicole received another delivery from Amazon. An in-line pool filter—a plastic jug essentially, with a hole in the bottom, a hole in the lid, and a mesh bag between the two. She packed this new purchase in her rucksack, beside the hand-held dust-buster, and headed out the door.

The weather was grim. Drizzle had set in from the small hours of the morning and hadn't let up. This was good though, it meant there'd be fewer people about.

Nicole drove out west, towards the woodland surrounding Limeworth, an old National Trust estate. She parked in a small passing place beside the country road, twenty or so metres shy of the gravel car park there, and continued on foot. She could see the car park was empty. She avoided entering the woodland through the car park as well though, favouring to swing right and walk along the edge of the neighbouring field while searching for an accessible way in. It didn't take long to find a place where the brambles fell short and nothing but a few low ferns stood between her and the well-trodden path beneath the venerable trees. She ducked through the undergrowth and began her soggy expedition.

There was no one about. The hardier dog walkers had evidently come and gone early, no leisurely walkers were out in this. With her hood up and head down, no one would have recognised her anyway.

A few hundred metres along the path, she saw the first signs of the cordon. Blue tape, much like police tape, was stretched across the path, secured by two sturdy trees. As she neared, Nicole could see the unmistakeable outline of the National Trust's oak leaf logo and walked slowly up to the sign. It was laminated and attached to a wooden clipboard, in turn attached to a wooden stake that had been hammered into the soft, wet ground.

Nicole stole a 360° glance around her, before turning back to the sign. It warned walkers to use the alternative path and to not allow dogs off leads here due to the discovery of a European Hornet nest.

The rest of the text went unread—Nicole had slipped under the tape and was cautiously treading along the edge of the path beyond. The low frequency hum had come as a surprise to her. Sure, she figured that these blighters made noise, but she hadn't known just how much.

She thought the rain would have subdued them somewhat, but it seemed to annoy them more. She could see more tape up ahead, concentrated around a single tree. The noise was intense already and Nicole was still a good fifteen metres away. She slipped her rucksack off her back and pulled on a mesh hood which sat atop her own jacket's hood. Then she removed the pool filter, dust-buster and heavy-duty rip tape. She took the flexible vacuum attachment and taped it to the bottom of the pool filter. Then she tore another piece of tape off ready for later, gently sticking it to the side of her bag.

Nicole stood up with this contraption in hand and began to approach the tree. One of the hornets landed on her jacket sleeve. She froze, although not from fright. More from curiosity and awe of being so close to such a nocuous creature. It too seemed merely curious, so she pressed on at a snail's pace.

Her precautionary measures were perhaps working after all. She'd been sceptical but figured it was worth a shot. She wore dark clothing—as if she'd have worn anything else. She had washed thoroughly with unscented soap—including washing her clothes in plain water to remove the detergent smells.

She was close enough to the tree now to see the nest. She could only see a small section, the gap in the side of the tree no more than eight inches wide. She guessed that the nest was considerably larger than this and likely filled the tree trunk. *That's a lot of hornets.*

It was at this point that Nicole became acutely aware of how utterly stupid this was. This was perhaps the most precarious a position she had put herself in since this whole thing started. *What. The. Actual...* Her thoughts berated her foolish actions, but she'd come this far now.

She switched on the dust-buster. The machine kicked into life. The startling sound exacerbated her sense of exposure. Nicole could feel the pull of the suction through the pool filter, the mesh bag inside shrinking against the force. The noise had perked up her European friends—there were definitely more of them now. She tried to stay very still and keep her breathing slow and steady—excess carbon dioxide being yet another trigger.

She tilted the filter opening towards one hornet that was resting on the dust buster. As it neared, the hornet could evidently sense the air change and fled. Nicole tried again with another that was resting on her sleeve but it too could sense the suction and flew off to safety.

This isn't going to work.

Nicole calculated that she'd be more successful where there was a denser concentration, and the longer she lingered, the more likely she'd have a nasty sting to contend with. So far, the extreme slow and calm motion was keeping the hornets from swarming, but they clearly weren't completely at ease.

She edged closer, the machine still droning, and reached out her left arm. The nozzle gradually approached an entry point to the left of the exposed nest. The nest was beige in colour but truly remarkable—the delicate swirls looked like whipped nougat. It made Nicole hanker for sugar.

Focusing her attention back on the hole, she slowly nudged the nozzle to fill the gap and cover the opening. She heard a change in the suction and could see one of the hornets in the mesh bag, followed by another. Within seconds the tally was up to four but the colony was noticeably perturbed. She kept the machine running, for fear of those she'd captured finding their way out again, and began to retreat.

A few were dive bombing at her face now, unable to get past the mesh hood. More were swarming the dust buster and the filter. She desperately wanted to leg it out of there but knew she couldn't fuck this up—*patience.*

She retraced her steps back to her discarded rucksack and crouched down, gently brushing away the ones that had landed on the back of her trouser legs. She grabbed the tape she'd prepared earlier and placed it over the filter hole, simultaneously switching off the vacuum.

Now with nothing but the drone of a thousand hornets, she could really appreciate the menace. She calmly placed the contraption in her backpack, zipped it up and slowly stood. They were slightly calmer now—out of sight, out of mind perhaps.

She was in no rush. She waited another few minutes before moving again, slowly moving back along the path edge, being mindful not to leave footprints, and made her way back to the main path. Each metre she traversed without incident, the fewer hornets troubled her.

There were none around her when she got back to the main path, but there was someone there waiting for her. A small terrier. Just sat there in the path staring at her, head cocked to one side.

Her eyes darted left and right, searching for the owner. A flash of red on her far right indicated she was soon to have company and she yanked the mesh hood from her face with frenzied worry. Like a child getting almost caught with its hand in the cookie jar.

The terrier just gazed at her, with indifference.

She bowed her head and walked with purpose towards the dog owner, as if she'd been storming along that path all the while. A curt, "Morning," was all that was proffered and all that was given in response.

What the fuck am I doing?

40

Well if she thought she'd had a lot of plates spinning before, it was nothing compared to the run up to Easter in the school calendar.

Not only was she planning a daring nighttime raid on Larry's Porsche Taycan, trying to find out all she could about this Cynthia Bishop without the old trout cottoning on, but she was also trying to construct an Easter bonnet for Alfie—one worthy of a prize, but not so good the teachers would guess she'd done it herself. She also had to find an outgrown uniform to donate to the PTA before term ended, remember to take a clean four-pint milk carton in before Tuesday, buy a red jumper for Alfie to wear for Red Nose Day Friday and book a parents' evening slot with grumpy Mrs Rowland.

It had been delicious news to find out that Dirty Larry drove an electric car—what could have been more perfect? One of Nicole's early assignments for GCHQ was to research and test such vehicles for vulnerabilities. As a branch of government, all departments were having pressure put on them to switch to electric vehicles and it was on special directive from Nicole's boss's boss to do all she could to demonstrate why that would be a spectacularly bad idea.

It had worked too.

Nicole was able to hack into any mid-range to high-end electric vehicle and control everything from the locking mechanisms to the steering. The implications were more frightening than the onslaught of drone technology.

The specific car that Larry drove was a '22 reg, Volcano Grey Porsche Taycan with an ostentatious red leather interior. He'd had it since new. Nicole had started driving a bizarre route out of town which took her northwest towards the railway line, past his house, then east to intercept the Falke Road and past the school where he worked. It was vital she was more than familiar with the routes.

The Easter holidays for mainstream schools were coming up next week and she'd already determined, through Mistlewaite Grange's website, that this public school had an extended holiday season that started the following week too, but went on for three weeks. There was a narrow window of opportunity here.

She'd brought the hornets back home with scarcely a bother. Once back, she'd taken the pool filter out of her bag and with a lot of care, managed to work the mesh bag loose inside so that they could fly around freely, safely inside the plastic jug-like filter. She had no intention of feeding them so hadn't bothered to do much research to that end. What she did know, though, was that, in a week's time they'd be starving. And enraged.

From the safety of her laptop, she had already begun to take control of the Taycan. There was something mischievous about watching the car park CCTV feed and then making the car—driverless—unlock itself. The headlights flashing to her over the CCTV feed, like a wink. She made the horn go off once and watched with amusement as the office staff came out to investigate and were none the wiser. Play time over.

40

She needed to bide her time.

* * *

Easter holidays had begun and her extended leave from the library meant long, playful days to spend with Alfie. Quality Mummy-Alfie time. All the while the creeping thoughts of what she needed to do soon were lurking in the back of her mind. But all in all she felt much happier nowadays.

Some concentrated research into Cynthia Bishop had given her a lot of good intelligence—things she could really play with and use. Most importantly, she had gotten eyes-on. She now knew what Cynthia Bishop looked like—she was taller than most women of her age, with coiffed, dark grey hair and a string of tiny red beads keeping tabs on her spectacles. She was always dressed well—decent tailoring, but nothing too showy or flamboyant. She seemed to have ingratiated herself deep into the town's community—volunteering at the church and being a notable member of the local am-dram group. She also ran coffee mornings every month to benefit a local mental health charity and a 'knit-n-natter' group that met at the Town Hall every third Tuesday of the month. Most interesting, though, were the group therapy sessions she ran at the Church Hall. These seemed to be free, two-hourly sessions where anyone could drop in, have a cup of tea and a biscuit and share, in confidence, anything that was troubling them. *A problem shared is a problem halved* read the tagline.

Despite living alone, Cynthia Bishop's ample abode, *Treetops*, boasted five bedrooms. She'd purchased it the year after Nicole had been shunted into her Laura Freeman life—living in a shitty ex-council maisonette near Milton Keynes. Nicole dug deep into some hidden online archives and found extensive photographs of the property from the previous sellers and even a virtual video tour, laying out all the rooms and their uses. There was a long narrow driveway, flanked by the single-storey part of the house on one side and the imposing hedges of the garden on the other. Entry to this drive was under a coachhouse arch. There were an awful lot of windows looking out on this drive. But there were other options, mused Nicole.

Cynthia's daughter Lucy, son-in-law Stuart, and their daughter Lily, lived in the town as well, but in a 60s-built chalet house. They visited *Treetops* often—at least they did that particular week.

A plan was starting to formulate in Nicole's mind now. And the more she tweaked and refined it, the more determined and angry she became.

Right now, she needed to focus on Larry, because these hornets wouldn't wait forever.

41

It was the last day of term for Mistlewaite Grange. There were a few boys who boarded, but almost all went home each day. This was the best opportunity Nicole would have for getting these hornets out of her house. Today, she knew where Larry was going to be, when he'd be leaving, and that he'd be alone. Alfie was at a friend's house for a sleepover. Nicole wasn't completely comfortable with this, not really knowing the parents that well, but she had to admit the timing was unbelievable.

After today she wouldn't get a chance like this again.

* * *

Nicole drove north towards Falke. It was 5:46 pm and the light was fading, but still far from dark. The drizzly weather was working in her favour though, bathing everything in a dreary dimness.

The Mistlewaite Grange gatehouse sat in the middle of a sweeping right-hand bend. Just before entering this bend, on the right, was a fairly nondescript hedge gap—presumably for farm vehicles to gain entry to that field. It was an ideal vantage point for Nicole. She monitored the school's CCTV feed from her laptop and watched as each teacher walked out to their vehicles and drove away. Moments later, the real-life version would appear from the driveway, its nose sticking out between the gateposts before launching left or right depending on whether the occupant was heading north towards Falke, or south towards Twynesham and beyond.

Nicole knew from her systems delve that Larry had a late management meeting with the two other faculty heads and Mr Coleridge. It was due to finish at 8:00 pm.

But Nicole wasn't waiting here for the meeting to end. She was just waiting for all the other staff members to make their way home, so she could hijack the feed and head into the secluded car park unseen.

There were five vehicles left now and the time was 6:57 pm. Number Six had left over half an hour ago and Nicole was getting impatient. The road was relatively busy and she didn't want to sit here any longer than she had to.

Her backpack sat on the passenger seat beside her and she gave it a gentle tap. The hornets made themselves known— the low buzzing had become something of a soothing sound between the whooshes of passing cars.

There was movement.

An older woman walked out to her Mini Countryman. Its headlights pierced the darkness, illuminating the front of the target Porsche parked opposite, as she swung out of her space towards the gate.

This is it.

The Mini appeared at the gate and turned left, heading away from where Nicole sat. Nicole made a few taps on her keyboard and the CCTV feed began its loop—the timer moving steadily onwards, the image portioned and displaying the same three minutes of inactivity over and over.

Nicole edged her hatchback out from her hiding place and joined the carriageway, abruptly swinging into the driveway opposite a moment later. She flicked off her headlights and wound down her window, listening for any unforeseen vehicles. She glided into the car park from the exit end, so she wouldn't need to drive past the administrative office windows where the meeting might be being held, and parked up beside the Porsche. Nicole straddled two spaces, despite their generosity, and was able to fully open her door without worry of touching the Porsche's door panel. She slipped out of her seat into a crouched position, using her driver's seat as a table for her laptop, her back to the Porsche.

A few more taps of the keyboard and she heard a faint click of a door mechanism releasing. She glanced left to check that the headlights she'd disabled remained dark. Satisfied, she reached over to lift her backpack from the passenger seat.

She'd thought a lot about how to get these hornets from the pool filter that they'd come to call home and into the cubby hole between the Porsche's front seats. Without wanting to risk a practice, she'd resorted to just blind hope and a bit of luck. She had one idea, but really, she'd need to just think on the fly.

She opened the Porsche's door and paused, half expecting the alarm to sound or the interior light to come on. She'd disabled both, so expected all to be dark and silent. She inwardly chastised herself for doubting her competence and pulled the door open with confidence. A waft of something expensive but brassy hit the back of her throat. *Fuck's sake, has he doused the fucking carpets with the stuff?* She leant across the driver's seat and opened the central compartment, flicking on her redlight head torch to reveal the assortment of collectables housed there, and was relieved to find it near empty. Just a couple of charging cables and a half-finished bag of Revels in evidence.

She retrieved the pool filter and its occupants from her bag and placed it beside her on the tarmac. She grabbed the halfeaten bag of Revels and emptied the remaining dozen nuggets into the palm of her glove. They all looked like coffee ones to her and she lobbed them sideways into the plants beyond.

She held the open end of the packet around the nozzle in the top of the pool filter and slipped out the intervening tape with a sideways yank. She nearly lost her grip on the packet, her gloves offering too little grip, but managed to hold it together.

The hornets needed no encouragement and were attracted to the sweet smell of the last occupants of the Revels packet. They all travelled through the nozzle within moments, gleeful that they'd finally found a way out.

Steeling herself for the next task, Nicole took a deep breath and pulled away the filter with her right hand whilst closing the packet with her left. They were trapped. Again.

The buzzing was louder now, and Nicole again questioned what on earth she was doing here. Her eyes remained fixed on the packet, as she lowered the filter and discarded it on top of her backpack. With both hands available now, she gave the opening of the packet a single twist—just enough, she reckoned, to allow her to drop it into the compartment and slam the lid closed, but not too much as to stop them from escaping the packet and not being ready for their special assignment.

Nicole went to do this now, leaning over the driver's seat and placing her left hand on the compartment lid. Her right hand

41

held the packet tightly—her hand beginning to ache from the pressure in her fingers. This position wasn't doing much for her back either, but she didn't want to be rubbing up against the interior and chance fibre transfer.

Her right hand lowered the packet into the compartment as her left began to close the lid. With lightning precision, she let go and slammed it closed. Breathing hard, she reversed herself out of the car, and returned to her crouched position. She could hear the hornets buzzing loudly in their new prison. Too loudly. This concerned her. If he heard them as soon as he got in the car then this could all be for nothing.

She'd have to do something about that.

It was then she noticed a second packet of half-eaten Revels, this time in the driver's door pocket. She emptied all but one Revel into her gloved hand and tossed them into the flowerbed with the others. The packet was returned to the door pocket.

Time now for a retreat. She packed up all the items in her backpack and tossed it onto her passenger seat. She checked her laptop: CCTV still looping. Time check—7:36 pm.

She closed the driver's door of the Porsche and moved around to the exposed side, keeping low and with her torch off. Another fleeting check around her and she opened the passenger door. Another waft of that God-awful cologne. Subconsciously she held her breath as she opened the glovebox and saw what she was looking for—an EpiPen carry case. The slender, unmistakable yellow case, was what she'd expected to find in the central compartment, but here it was. She grabbed out the pen inside, flicked off the blue cap and injected the epinephrine into the ground before replacing the cap, fastening the carry case and laying it back in the glovebox. She was surprised to only find one pen inside.

She closed the door again and headed back to her own driver's door, climbed in and—as silently as she could—vacated the car park back the way she'd entered.

She made it back to her hedge-front hidey-hole and reopened the laptop, returning the CCTV feed back to normal and making a few minor adjustments to the Porsche's start-up programming.

Then waited.

42

Dear Lord that old todger hasn't a fucking clue how to run this school... bloody good job too I suppose, thought Lawrence, as he collected up his belongings and headed out of his first-floor office.

The complete ineptitude of Mr Coleridge was the primary reason for accepting this job in the first place. He was essentially able to do what he pleased—to whomever he pleased—and this doddery septuagenarian hadn't the wherewithal to even notice.

For years Lawrence Rackham-Hush had been allowed to run the school by proxy—using Coleridge as a front. Responding to and signing letters as him, able to ward off complaints and lie to parents and students about all sorts—whatever kept him free and unhindered.

Brimming with his own superiority, he flicked off the light to his office and stepped out into the dark corridor. He loved the school at night with hardly anyone about and the boys who boarded here few and easily preyed upon. *Poor little Francis misses his Mummy, waa waa waa.* Lawrence smirked at some unbidden memory.

There was no time for a dormitory visit this evening though. The wife wanted him home for some gala event her offices were funding—another empty gesture at trying to keep the county's justice system working in their favour. Schmoozing judges tonight was not what Lawrence wanted to be doing.

Coleridge was driving off as he descended the steps into the staff car park.

Striding over to his car, the headlights came on—just the proximity of the key was enough to wake his Gertie up. He always named his cars, even as a young adult. And always elderly ladies' names—something for the shrinks to interpret.

He opened the car door and dropped himself into the driver's seat, throwing his leather satchel across to the passenger seat and pulling his door closed behind him. The interior light flicked off, which was strange and the radio sprang into life— BBC Radio 3 blasting out Franz Schubert. Lawrence tried the off button to silence the deafening choral chanting but the damn thing wouldn't shut off.

He was able to lower the volume though, at least enough to be able to hear himself think. *I don't have bloody time for this bollocks.* He started the engine and rammed home his seatbelt. He glanced at the clock. *Shit I'm late.*

The Porsche leapt forward towards the driveway, the powerful electric engine pushing his body into the moulded seat. He smiled. He loved that feeling—the power, the force.

He swung out of the gateway, barely considered giving way, and headed north. As he wound his way towards home, he tried once more to change the radio station, lower the volume, turn the thing off. None of it worked. *Piece of shit radio...140 grand for fuck's sake.* Einaudi's *Questa Notte* came on next. The purposeful piano resonance overwhelmed the small car.

As he swung left, west towards Brook House, his stomach growled. He was starving and *this fucking gala dinner will be nothing but shitty amuse-bouche bollocks.* He plunged his right hand into the door pocket. *One fucking Revel?* He tossed it into his mouth and went on the hunt for more. Keeping watch on the road ahead. He pulled open the central compartment to search there.

What the f... his inner thoughts trailed off as he heard a chaotic and terrifying hum. He felt something brush his cheek. He panicked. He let go of the wheel, his foot came off the pedal, as he flailed around in the driver's seat desperate to get away from the unmistakeable buzzing of more than one massive wasp. His thoughts went wild and filled with desperation. The car had drastically slowed but rolled on at a steady 20 mph, not stopping, holding a straight line. Lawrence didn't really notice—the rhythmic piano emanating from the speakers at odds with the situation.

His vision was unfocused and, in the dim light, he could only make out shadows of things zooming past his face. He knew he should remain calm, to get out of the vehicle, but that was proving difficult. He yanked on the inner door handle but nothing happened, the car kept moving and the door disobeyed.

Dazzling headlights illuminated the interior, as an approaching vehicle failed to dim its lights. The full beams created haunting shadows everywhere he looked. The van approached. *Quesa Notte* was intensifying now and the headlights were blinding. He wasn't even attempting to control his car any longer, but somehow it managed to pull neatly into a passing place to allow the oncoming van to pass. Lawrence pounded at the windows for help, unable to lower them, as the other driver passed by without noticing the frantic cries from the car beside him.

The Porsche pulled back into the road and took the next left turn down a narrow, single-track lane, then became motionless. All the while the occupant was thrashing about and screaming. Lawrence's vision narrowed as his heart rate spiked, or was it the lights went out? He felt something land on his neck and he went berserk with a new found level of horror, clawing at it, desperate to get it off his skin. Unintentionally, he had trapped it between two of his fingers which was when the stinger found flesh. Instinctively, Lawrence crushed the insect from the injected pain and let it fall from his hand. A sting in his neck was worsening. The searing pain was shooting in throngs from his fleshy jowls and spreading fast. His hand was swelling up. The intensity of the song matched his dread. The volume rising. He wailed in agony and fear—fear of knowing precisely what was coming. The itching was so awful he clawed at his neck leaving angry red stripes with his fingernails. His eyes and face began to swell. His throat felt thick and his tongue heavy. He was wheezing now, frantically sucking in each breath. He grabbed for the steering wheel, pulling himself upright. With his right hand, he pulled on the inner door handle again and again; he couldn't fathom why it wouldn't open. He turned the other way, reaching for the glovebox. His eyes all but swollen shut, he fumbled with the carry case, and almost dropped the EpiPen as he flicked off the blue cap. The pen found his thigh, but nothing happened. His hand went limp. The EpiPen fell to his lap. His legs kicked out with the agony, writhing around in his moulded seat, powerless against the infuriated hornets. He was weeping now. Hopelessness flooded his body and he stopped struggling with the door. His will dissipated with each descending bar of score. He was going to die—he knew he was going to die and yet... *I don't deserve this.* As the final twenty seconds of *Questa Notte* pounded through his ears, Lawrence thought of his dog.

43

It turned out to be his wife who found him. She'd been expecting Lawrence home and the journey was not far. He wasn't answering his phone so she had decided to drive out to the school to find him and drag him home. She was furious at being made late for the gala.

She'd spotted his car parked to the side of the road, just a quarter mile from their home. The doors were all unlocked, the lights on, the windows closed. He was slumped in the driver's seat, still warm, his face red and swollen, and his hands the same. An expended EpiPen lay in his lap.

The flying culprit, or culprits, had fled the scene.

It had been too late to help him, although she'd tried. Valiantly, but hopelessly, she'd tried.

44

The very next day, with Alfie still at his friends house, Nicole set in motion a series of events that she hoped would finally give her the freedom she craved—the freedom she deserved.

It was impossible to control all the variables sometimes. But she had to do something, and the longer she delayed, the bigger the threat to Alfie's safety and their future.

Nicole hadn't slept well. Her face was stone, her mind fixed and unwavering. This war had been brought to her door and she had fought heroically, but always at a disadvantage.

The tables were turning. Her opponent had no idea what was coming, and there was immense power in that. If she struck now, her rival should be off-guard and unsuspecting.

It was time to take the fight to *her* door.

45

Cynthia's day was much like every other had been recently. In fact, week-on-week was pretty much the same—only the seasons changed and the number of funerals went up.

She was an active woman. Kept herself busy. "A busy mind is a happy mind," her father used to say. And Cynthia lived by this rule. When she moved to Twynesham a few years ago, she moved to be closer to her daughter and family. Her daughter Lucy was already living and working in the town at the time of her retirement. It was a natural choice to leave her hectic job in the Big Smoke and relocate to sleepy Norfolk. Cynthia had adored her quaint flat south of the river, although she had barely spent enough time in it to be sufficiently affected by its failings. And now she'd sold up and moved away, she'd never be able to see it for what it really was.

Despite the deficiencies, the flat sold for substantially more than the asking price. Cynthia was overjoyed at the offer, which enabled her to cash-buy a stunning, palatial property in the oldest part of Twynesham. Sure the house was far too big for just her, but she'd always dreamt of having an open fireplace, space for an indecently humongous Christmas tree and a dedicated room for her painting.

The fact that she could buy this place outright and bequeath it to her daughter and family later, made the deal all the more sweet.

Cynthia was pondering that morning's class whilst the pot boiled. She roamed from room to room tidying away the odd item that she found to be not quite in its proper place—these were few and far between. She finished making her clementine tea, slipped on her Land Rover green Crocs that sat on the camel-hair doormat, and took a step out into the sun-drenched spring garden. It had been beckoning her out there and she was all too happy to oblige. Tea in hand, she unhurriedly circled the flowerbeds in an anti-clockwise manner, letting the sun warm her as she dead-headed with her right hand and sipped tea with her left. Her mind was so awake. Every sound and feeling felt fresh and engaging. She watched the bees as they travelled from flower to flower, collecting their daily quota. And gave a passing thought to Lawrence Rackham-Hush. She begrudgingly stooped down to yank out a new shoot of dandelion and then went on—her knees unhappy with the sudden extra load.

As she performed her tranquil task, her passing thought of Lawrence developed into musings on the previous year's events.

For too long she had wrestled with the notion that her darling Alex was forever immortalised as a victim of bad luck, whilst that disgusting, worthless libertine still drew breath. *Why wasn't he drinking himself to death?* He appeared locked in his own purgatory, never able to drink enough to put us *all* out of his misery. She'd seen to that. Finally. The authorities had let her down—had let them all down—and she'd vowed to fix it. She had spent much of that time infiltrating and ingratiating herself wherever she could, establishing an exemplary reputation as a community-centric, moral and upstanding citizen. Her varied and numerous commitments were all meticulously structured to provide iron-clad alibis. She'd worked so hard and put in so much effort.

She moved away from the rose beds. *And then there was Sophie.* It had been kismet. Cynthia didn't much believe in all that claptrap but she had to admit that the appearance of Sophie Baxter in her very own Twynesham was too splendid a coincidence to ignore. *These azaleas need attention.*

Cynthia had known just what Sophie's pressure points were and how to tunnel into that fragile, damaged mind to exploit all those deliciously heinous skills. All her plans from the previous eighteen months had been dropped. But Cynthia wasn't sorry. This was altogether far more auspicious.

It was destiny that had brought them together in this post-agency life and Cynthia wasn't about to let this opportunity pass by without attempting to take full advantage of it.

Her thoughts returned to her garden at that moment—the half eaten leaves of her treasured dianthus had interrupted her reflections. She'd not been much of a gardener until she'd moved here, for obvious reasons, but she'd taken to it like a duckling to a pond. She'd systematically replaced thoughts of psychoanalysis and board reports with those of Latin binomial nomenclature and flowering periods.

The warmth of the sun on her back was soothing and it was only a few minutes before she let go of her tightly wound cardigan and allowed the waterfall folds to flap in the breeze. She could hear the sound of the odd car that passed by the front of the house but other than that, nothing but nature. A lifetime in London had deprived her of so much, but now she was free from so many burdens: financial, mental and now, emotional.

Thanks to Sophie. Or should she say, Nicole.

And hadn't it been wickedly wonderful? She had to admit she was delighted at the end result and would be forever in Nicole's debt. The gratitude she felt was overpowering and lately had the consequence of causing her to temporarily forget the malicious nature of its coming about. But the means to the end was not without its residual risk. The problem she now faced was one of self-preservation. She knew full well that she had no further need to cause the girl any more undue stresses or bother, now that the deed was done. There were only ever going to be the three. But how could she let Nicole know this without giving away her own identity?

Her thoughts turned to the possible books in that useful little library that might somehow do the job for her. One last hurrah to cap it all off. Rather poetic one thought.

But maybe I've opened Pandora's box here and she doesn't forget—and she seeks me out? The thought was unsettling, and for a fleeting moment, Cynthia felt exposed. Observed. She straightened and let go of the rose head she was cradling in her hand. She glanced around the garden perimeter, not quite sure what she was expecting to find, but checking nonetheless. Pulling her cardigan back around her to ward off the uncomfortable chill that was travelling up her spine, she walked back towards the kitchen door, slightly faster than necessary, and locked the door behind her.

Maybe I can't leave it after all. She'd had hardly any time to fully scope out a game plan before putting it into action and the exit strategy hadn't been considered at all. She was regretting this failing on her part. She was coming round to the idea that she would need to turn her attention to Nicole and what she could do to silence her forever without revealing her identity

45

and connection when she spotted it.

It was resting on the end table between the rugged and worn antique blue Chesterfield and the over-stuffed Balmoral-check armchair—the dazzling yellow cover contrasting against the dove grey, muted furnishings. She was inspired to paint the scene but the heaviness in her heart eclipsed all else.

In the split second that followed, she had considered every decision she'd ever made, whether she had spent enough time with her daughter and granddaughter over the past few years, and also weighed up the options that befell her now. To run, to hide, to fight, to bother panicking, to call for help.

She observed the room anew, trying to recall whether anything here right now was amiss. Nothing else seemed to be, but then, her thumping heart and rush of adrenaline were preventing her from thinking clearly. Her trembling limbs were making her unsteady. She was going to fall.

She gingerly moved across the space towards the book and, as she did so, realised she knew it. She recognised it, and for the briefest of moments the terror subsided and she was sure that this was just one of her own books that she'd simply forgotten she left there. But then she didn't tend to borrow books from the library and this was clearly a library book, with its clear plastic cover and index labels on the spine.

She leant over the table, hands clasped beneath her bosom, and looked down past her nose, as if she were leaning across the opening of a dirty toilet to peer inside, knowing it was going to be unpleasant.

She didn't need to pick this book up. Despite not actually reading it herself, she knew what it was about. And she knew just what it meant too.

46

Cynthia spent some minutes standing by the end table, considering her position.

Nicole has figured out who I am. She hadn't the faintest idea how she could've done it but done it she had. Now Cynthia was fucked. She wasn't one for using foul language, but there were a few occasions when it was warranted and this was most definitely one.

Jules, Cynthia's long-haired Maine Coon, brushed up against her leg and startled her out of her trance. *I never hear that damn cat coming,* the giant tufted paws were stealthy. There was a sound from the old barn door that separated this single-storey part of the house from the rest—the unmistakable sound of an ancient hinge creaking against itself. Cynthia gasped and spun round to face the noise as Jules bolted, bashing her back against the cat flap with such force as she did so, it broke the catch.

Framed within the right-hand portion of the double oak door was Sophie. Nicole.

The two women just stared at one another. Cynthia could hardly breathe, her chest was tightening and her head swam. She couldn't think straight and her feet were like lead.

It was Nicole who spoke first.

"How dare you?" Her voice was steady and imperious. Cynthia couldn't respond.

"Who the fuck do you think you are? Playing with people's hearts and minds...and *lives* like this?"

Still, Cynthia remained silent. Her mind wasn't as sharp as it once had been and she was struggling to process her thoughts and options quickly enough to reply before Nicole spoke again.

"I don't know how you thought you were going to get away with this? I can only presume that you had some master plan to finally do away with me and silence me forever."

By God, I wish I really had.

Cynthia's tongue felt thick. She still couldn't think of anything to say—she was caught completely off guard and didn't relish the feeling one jot.

Nicole continued before she could think of what was best to say next.

"You have de-rooted such harmful thoughts and memories over the past months and," Nicole's voice faltered, "you put my little boy's life in danger, as well as my own. I can't forgive that. I just can't let you have this hold over me. I don't know what you have planned next."

Neither do I!

"But I am taking control of this now. This all stops. Today."

There was a pause as Nicole waited for some sort of reply, but none came. Cynthia had barely moved a muscle. She was frantically thinking of a way out of all this but was coming up empty. Her tongue no longer felt thick, but it was beginning to sting and it caused her brow to furrow as her hand travelled up towards her mouth to examine further. This had not escaped Nicole's attention.

"Do you want to know what I think? I think the agency did

almost as much of a number on you as they did me—only in a different way. You might think you were in control and whatever, but really they were using you. They used and used—made you into a sour, apathetic old woman who lost the ability to see the value in others' lives. You are selfish. And right about now your lips and tongue are starting to burn."

True enough, half a minute ago Cynthia's tongue had begun to heat up like she'd eaten chillies—she hated chillies. Her lips were burning too now, and she felt the urge to swallow—her mouth watering profusely.

She looked up at Nicole. Cynthia was always so good at reading people and seeing their emotions plastered on their faces, but she couldn't read Nicole. Was it a smirk? Pity? Dread set in and a wave of heat washed over Cynthia like a fever. She shivered.

Nicole spoke again. "Started sweating yet?"

She spoke with such nonchalance as if she was merely asking her whether it was going to rain later.

"What have you done to me?" Cynthia blurted out, finally finding her voice but feeling every bit of her elderly fragility.

"I'm silencing you... Cynthia."

Cynthia was fairly certain no one had ever spoken her name with such distaste before. She was sweating though—a lot. She shrugged off her cardigan, letting it fall to the floor.

"It's not a question of morality at this point, Cynthia, but prudence. I'm sure you understand. It'll only be a minute or so and you won't be able to speak any longer. So if you have something important you want to say, now would be the time."

Cynthia was rather taken aback by this. *Last words? Am I dying? She'll never get away with this.*

"You'll never get away wi...," her throat stopped her midway.

46

"You sure about that? I think you'll find that I've dedicated a little more time to get my ducks in a row—more time than you evidently have bothered with. And when this all gets investigated, someone clever *might* work out your involvement in an ongoing diplomatic issue with the agency right now. One concerning a Russian informant that you were very closely connected with—in a professional capacity of course.

"A diplomatic issue where your unwelcome interference has put some rather high-up bods' noses right out of joint. That clever person might well check a few things—like your online presence, your digital footprint. They might even check your shed. And ultimately arrive at the conclusion that your duplicitous interference pissed off the wrong people.

"That same someone clever might just put together all the meagre breadcrumbs I have left them. And they'll all lead to you. They certainly won't be looking for me."

Nicole advanced towards her. Cynthia backed away, but her foot caught on her abandoned cardigan and she stumbled into the back of the armchair.

Nicole spoke again as she travelled the distance between them.

"I suppose it's only fair to let you know what to expect. In a few more minutes, you'll start having seizures. They'll get progressively worse over the next couple of hours as your body begins to shut down. It's not nice, I admit, but this TTX stuff is *the* weapon of choice for a lot of Kremlin agents at the moment. Maybe they got a BOGOF deal or something." Nicole gave a little shrug.

"You'll be lucid all the while—which I think is rather impressive to be honest. The whole thing will take about six hours. There's no cure, no antidote. You're in it for the ride now Cynthia."

Nicole was by her side now. Cynthia wanted to lash out, to wallop Nicole square in the face and run from this place, out into the sunshine and safety. But she felt so desperately sad. She couldn't do anything but stare at her. Her fate was decided and there was nothing she could do. Someone must come for her. It could not end like this. She remembered she had her class this morning. Someone would come looking for her. Nicole sensed her anticipated salvation.

She prodded Cynthia near her collarbone and she fell ungainly onto the Chesterfield as the first seizure took hold. As Cynthia's body trembled and struggled against the seizing muscles, Nicole's voice cut through the ringing in her ears.

"I've taken the liberty of cancelling all your appointments for today—even the tea date you have with someone named Harriet at 10. Everyone thinks you're feeling a bit peaky and won't be bothering you until tomorrow at least. So that's one less thing to fret about, eh?"

But Cynthia couldn't answer—she could only struggle and writhe with each worsening seizure, feeling her body systematically shut down, and experiencing every agonising minute. Nicole had nothing left to say it seemed. She stood now, silently, in the space between the armchair, the coffee table and the picture window. Just standing and watching. Waiting.

The time ticked by and Cynthia's head whirled with thoughts and desperate prayers. She was so very regretful in that last hour, acknowledging that the regret was surely as much for getting caught as it was for doing these things to Nicole in the first place.

The weather had turned after a couple of hours—the sky darkened as rain clouds rolled in from the south-east. The

46

light in the house was dim and colourless. Still, Nicole stood vigil, waiting.

The last sound Cynthia heard was the heavy rainfall on the skylight above and the mewing of Jules, left out in the rain.

Epilogue

It had been a year to the day since Nicole had set herself free.

Her ruse had succeeded. Cynthia Bishop was found unresponsive in her home that same day by a busy-body friend who had been unable to reach her by phone. She was later pronounced dead by the attending paramedics whilst they transported her to Blyworth's Critical Care Unit.

A major incident was declared the following day, after Blyworth University Hospital staff sent samples for testing. The Defence, Science and Technology Laboratory at Porton Down confirmed the substance used was a nerve agent, and a murder investigation was launched.

It didn't take the authorities long to investigate. Willingness to devote resources was high. They discovered that the primary source of contamination was Cynthia Bishop's newest batch of clementine tea—a blend that she had developed in her own garden shed. They had found multiple contamination sites in there, and further testing by the Organisation for the Prohibition of Chemical Weapons confirmed the UK findings that TTX nerve agent had been the cause of death.

TTX, or tetrodotoxin, was a poison found in puffer fish and blue-ringed octopuses. There had been countless reports from agents operating out of Russia and the neighbouring Baltic countries, the robust intelligence suggested that TTX was being heavily researched for wider deployment by the Russian GRU military intelligence agency.

All the meticulously laid breadcrumbs were being followed to the letter. Nicole felt more relief with each passing day. The days became weeks, the weeks became months. The breadcrumbs led authorities to a road they didn't have clearance to travel down. The case would remain perpetually unsolved.

* * *

Tracey Wolston was not mourned. With no friends to speak of and distant family members abroad, only three people attended her funeral.

The care home in Dunwell thrived. The new manager was promoted from within the existing staff and brought with them a strong desire to lead by example. The morning room was converted back into a communal living space for the residents. The plush green carpet had been replaced with hard flooring, and all traces of the horrific ordeal were now only memories.

The morning room's door was left open these days—although that never stopped the new manager from recalling the trepidation she had felt whenever she had needed to knock on it.

* * *

Robert Lock continued to farm Blacklock Farm alone, accompanied only by the dutiful Rebel. Life was quiet and simple. Just as he wanted it.

His brother's ashes were scattered in the woods beside Regent's Field. The Midrakes would inherit it all one day. They had already brokered a deal with the last remaining Lock. The ancestral rivalries were finally put to bed. Robert welcomed the buy-out deal. It gave him fewer worries and lessened his burden. Whilst he still could, he would farm Blacklock Farm alone. And when he could no longer manage that, he'd be permitted to remain in the farmhouse whilst the Midrakes took over farming the land.

So for now, Robert lived peacefully and with a modicum of happiness for his lot.

* * *

Helena Rackham-Hush was thoroughly enjoying her new widowed life. It had been devastating to find Lawrence in that state, but then it would have been equally as devastating to find anybody in that state. And she wasn't one to dwell on things too long. Not when they ultimately gave her piece of mind.

Her career was on the up but she had always felt an unsettled suspicion about Lawrence's predisposed fancies. She was acutely aware that the scrutiny that would come hand-in-hand with her taking the silk would risk exposure of his past. A past so scandalous it would have the power to lay ruin to everything she had worked for her entire adult life.

She viewed this tragic accident as a gift from above and vowed

EPILOGUE

to make the most of her new-found, carefree, freedom.

***

Nicole continued to work at the library—practically full-time these days—and enjoyed it immensely. Her aptitude for the role was evident and her lack of genuine qualifications never came into the picture. She found herself ready to embrace the social connections the job offered and, for the first time in her adult life, she had made a friend.

In the days leading up to Cynthia's death, Nicole had spent hours combing the agency's servers. She was meticulous. Identifying and removing any and all traces of *Sophie*, *SB99* and *Laura* from the records. Her previous life existed only in the memories of those who had witnessed it first-hand.

Alfie was doing very well at school—an avid reader like his mum. His social life was ever-expanding, forcing hers to do likewise. The pair adored their time together. They had thoroughly settled into their middling life in the middling little town of Twynesham.

One day, she knew she would have to answer questions about who Alfie's father was, but for now, she could live her life in relative peace. The secret safe.

After all, two *can* keep a secret, if one of them is dead.

Afterword

My mother wrote a book.

She started in 2015 and was still tweaking and refining it until a few weeks before she passed away. She'd spent years building a complex plot, dozens of inter-connecting characters and one hundred and forty thousand words. It took two more years, and extensive assistance from a family friend, to get the book ready for publication.

It was during this time that the idea for *this* book came to be...

In the months following Mum's passing, I was struggling to even begin reading her manuscript. There were many pestering me to get going with it, as they were keen to see her work published. But there was something tangible holding me back from starting. Once I'd read all her words there would be nothing left for her to say to me. There was a finality to it that I was evidently trying to avoid.

So it was, when my guiding light in the form of family friend Jan, had instructed the book cover designer and I needed to put my big girl pants on. Trouble was, I was trying to brief a cover designer to create a cover for a book I hadn't read more than three chapters of, six years previously. Jan filled in the majority of the brief and, although riddled with spoilers, was still just a straw-man version of events. The problem with that is it leaves ample room for interpretation ... and I added two to

AFTERWORD

two and got five.

In the weeks thereafter I caught up with my reading and discovered that what I had assumed about Mum's primary character and her background was entirely wrong. I thought her leading character was going to reveal herself to be this kick-ass, gritty, ex-agent with a shady past full of missions and clandestine operations in exotic places. I was looking forward to reading about this menopausal retired widow who had once been a Jane Bond. A super spy. With unrivalled, but buried, skills that would surprise even her close friends and daughters. But that's not what Mum had written.

I was a bit disappointed. I got over it ... but a seed of something had been planted.

It was the morning of 14 September 2022, I only partly woke from my nights sleep, continuing a half-conscious dream. A thirty-something woman working in a library, periodically finding cryptic notes on makeshift bookmarks tucked into books of significance—all providing clues. She's running from something, and someone knows what. There's dread and intrigue—and a dark past. I was fully awake now. Clinging onto the tails of this half-dream trying to remember it all long enough to write it down. I snatched my phone from the bedside table and, bleary-eyed, began to type a note.

Within three months I'd written half of it. Granted it's a short book, but still. The words poured out of me. The process was cathartic. I didn't have much of a plan—just a series of three people concealing the *real* motive, and a blackmailer who knew more than they should about our protagonist.

It may not be considered much. I spent a relatively short

amount of time on it and didn't feel particularly motivated to pick it apart to any considerable degree, nor add in thousands of extra words just to hit some arbitrary ideal-novel-length quota. I was satisfied with the level of detail, the pace of the read and the length of the chapters. I didn't want to get to the point where I was sick to the back teeth of my own words, or fatigued with over-editing. I wanted to enjoy the process from start to finish.

I've been asked about Twynesham a fair few times. I can't deny that those of you familiar with Aylsham in North Norfolk could certainly draw many comparisons, and even go as far as being able to orientate oneself from the text to the real geography of the town. Mum always said, "Write what you know." Well I know Aylsham... so figured it was as good a place as any to start. I know which real houses each of my characters live in, and what their places of work look like. I can see the library, with its vertical blinds, and walk up to the church, with its non-existent pigeon problem.

As for the characters, they aren't based on anyone I know. I'm thankful for that. I certainly wouldn't want to know any of the key characters of the book, although I do think Nicole and I would get along. Oddly enough, many of her observed annoyances are shared by me. And I reckon she'd have the skill to sort out my glitchy WiFi.

You can learn many things whilst researching a book. One enduring lesson I shall carry with me from this moment on is one I shall leave you with now:

Be wary of pharmacists—they know *a lot.*

About the Author

Lauren Newbrook doesn't write books. Well technically that's not true—she clearly does—this one. But she doesn't normally. Normally she's an ordinary working mother living in a middling town in the northern region of beautiful rural Norfolk. It just so happens that one day she had an idea and wanted to write it down.

Lauren is something of a creative jack-of-all-trades. Never particularly excelling in any one medium, rather preferring to dabble in whatever takes her fancy. But what she lacks in writing credentials, she more than makes up for in drama, intrigue, and pace.

Before settling down, she and her husband-to-be took a seven month overland trip around Africa, and she wrote an extensive blog along the way detailing their adventures for those back home. They encouraged Lauren to write more, and sowed a seed that never completely dissipated. It took a while, but hopefully they'll consider it worth the wait.

Printed in Great Britain
by Amazon